"I Need You

Emily looked into his ⬜ never in her life had sh⬜ ⬜ this way.

"I'm going home tomorrow, Zach."

"We have tonight," he answered. He picked her up and carried her to the family room, where he closed the door and slipped the bolt in place.

He eased her down and with a powerful sweep of his arms he yanked off his T-shirt and tossed it aside, muscles rippling. She inhaled deeply. She saw his intention as he bent his head to kiss her, and she did not want to stop him. She sensed the vulnerability in him and she wanted to give to him, to make him feel complete. At the same time, she didn't want to go home with a broken heart. It was a fleeting thought, whisked away by his fingers and his mouth and his body. This moment she was willing to risk all....

Dear Reader,

August predictably brings long steamy days…and hot sensuous nights. And this month Silhouette Desire spotlights the kind of pure passion that can erupt only in that sizzling summer climate.

Get ready to fall head over heels for August's MAN OF THE MONTH, a sexy rancher who opens his home (and his heart?) to a lost beauty desperately hoping to recover her memory in *A Montana Man* by Jackie Merritt. Bestselling author Cait London continues her hugely popular miniseries THE TALLCHIEFS with *Rafe Palladin: Man of Secrets*. Rafe is an irresistible takeover tycoon with a plan to *acquire* a Tallchief lady. Barbara McMahon brings readers the second story in her IDENTICAL TWINS! duo—in *The Older Man* an exuberant young woman is swept up by her love and desire for a tremendously gorgeous, *much* older man.

Plus, talented Susan Crosby unfolds a story of seduction, revenge and scandal in the continuation of THE LONE WOLVES with *His Seductive Revenge*. And TEXAS BRIDES are back with *The Restless Virgin* by Peggy Moreland, the story of an innocent Western lady tired of waiting around for marriage—so she lassos herself one unsuspecting cowboy! And you've never seen a hero like *The Consummate Cowboy*, by Sara Orwig. He's all man, all-around ornery and all-out tempted…by his ex-wife's sister!

I know you'll enjoy reading all six of this sultry month's brand-new Silhouette Desire novels by some of the most beloved and sexy authors of romance.

Regards,

Melissa Senate

Melissa Senate
Senior Editor
Silhouette Books

Please address questions and book requests to:
Silhouette Reader Service
U.S.: 3010 Walden Ave., P.O. Box 1325, Buffalo, NY 14269
Canadian: P.O. Box 609, Fort Erie, Ont. L2A 5X3

SARA ORWIG
THE CONSUMMATE COWBOY

SILHOUETTE *Desire*™

Published by Silhouette Books

America's Publisher of Contemporary Romance

SILHOUETTE BOOKS

ISBN 0-373-76164-3

THE CONSUMMATE COWBOY

Copyright © 1998 by Sara Orwig

This edition published by arrangement with Harlequin Books S.A.

® and TM are trademarks of Harlequin Books S.A., used under license.
Trademarks indicated with ® are registered in the United States Patent
and Trademark Office, the Canadian Trade Marks Office and in other
countries.

Printed in U.S.A.

Books by Sara Orwig

Silhouette Desire

Falcon's Lair #938
The Bride's Choice #1019
A Baby for Mommy #1060
Babes in Arms #1094
Her Torrid Temporary Marriage #1125
The Consummate Cowboy #1164

Silhouette Intimate Moments

Hide in Plain Sight #679

SARA ORWIG

is a national bestselling author with six *Romantic Times* awards, including Love and Laughter and a Career Achievement Award for Contemporary Fiction. Sara's books have been translated into more than twenty languages, and she loves getting letters from readers around the world. An avid reader, Sara loves her native Oklahoma with its hot summers and gardening opportunities. Jalapeño peppers are the latest specialty that Sara and husband, David, are growing. The yard is filled with plants and the house is filled with books, as well as some people very special to Sara.

Thanks to Pat Froehle and to Debra Robertson

Prologue

"Things cannot get worse," Emily Stockton said aloud. Later she would remember her foolhardy prediction. She turned off the faucets, stepped out of the shower and wrapped her red hair in a towel. Exhausted from working a ten-hour day at the office of Chicago Charities, she dried quickly and yanked on a short blue cotton nightgown. As she slipped it over her head, she heard the ring of the phone.

"Oh, no!" She could imagine Meg Dodson calling about the adoption they had been working on for weeks. She hurried to the phone and picked up the receiver, bracing for more upheaval and Meg's panicky voice. An unintelligible and hysterical female voice ran words together.

"Meg? Slow down. I can't understand you at all."

"Emily, it's me—Amber. I'm in desperate trouble. Help me. You've got to help me. He's after me—"

"Amber?" Emily frowned in shock, trying to remember the last time she had talked to her sister. She shook her head, wondering what Amber's latest predicament was. Her sister had already gone through two husbands and was now married to the third.

"You've got to help me. I know you'll come, but please be careful. If he knows you're going to help me, you'll be in danger. I've got to get away from him—"

"Who's him? Raimundo? Zach Durham?" Amber's current husband and most recent ex seemed the logical possibilities. The first had long ago disappeared from Amber's life.

"You know how tough Zach is and how he hates me. Stay away from him!"

"Amber, you're not making sense. Who's after you?"

"I've got to go. I think he's here. I'm in New Mexico. Up north. I'll call you—"

The phone clicked, and Emily stared at the receiver. "Damn," she said, half tempted to hang up, go to bed, and forget all about Amber and her problems. Her sister had been in trouble all of Emily's life. Yet Amber sounded more frightened than ever before. With a sigh of resignation, Emily knew she would have to do something. No matter what kind of jams her family got themselves into, she always felt compelled to stand by them. She was the youngest member of the family, yet she'd always felt like the oldest.

As she blew dry her hair, pulling the brush through her thick reddish-golden hair, the curls springing back in an annoying tangle, she mulled over Amber's call. She hadn't taken a vacation in three years. She could wind up the latest adoption and ask for time off to go to New Mexico and see what help Amber needed. She didn't know *where* in northern New Mexico, but she expected another wild call from Amber. And more than likely, the trouble involved Amber's second husband, Zach Durham, who was a rancher in New Mexico. Otherwise, why would Amber be in that state? The last call Emily had received from her sister had been from Acapulco, where Amber was celebrating her latest marriage to Raimundo Morales. That had been eight months ago. Maybe Raimundo and Zach were fighting over Amber.

Although Emily knew she could use some time off work, she didn't want to spend it tied up with Amber's problems. But she also knew she couldn't ignore Amber's plea for help. She let out a long sigh.

"Chump," she grumbled into the empty darkness.

One

How long can someone live after a rattlesnake bite? Emily wondered. It hadn't happened yet, but she half expected to hear a sinister rattle at any moment or feel fangs sink into her ankle. Now she wished she had worn boots instead of sneakers.

"Ouch!" She bit her lip and yanked her sleeve free from the barbed-wire fence. A perfect place for dying, she thought morbidly. Wind whistled through the regal aspen, their white trunks pale in the July moonlight, as she ignored a No Trespassing sign and climbed between the strands of the fence into a forbidden pasture.

Spruce and aspen cast black shadows across the ground and she could imagine various deadly threats hidden in the darkness. Like snakes. She loathed them. She had also seen pictures of bulls on the property, and prayed there wasn't one in her vicinity. And out here in the wilds of New Mexico, there could be mountain lions, wild dogs, wild pigs.

She preferred the streets of Chicago any night to walking alone here.

Looking back across the fence, she saw her car pulled off the side of the divided highway and parked in the shadows of a spruce.

Remember why you're here, she reminded herself as she moved cautiously along the fence, heading toward the road that passed through wide, locked gates.

For a quarter of a mile along the highway in either direction from the ranch's secured gates stretched chain-link fencing. Not a friendly place. A chill ran down Emily's spine. Zach Durham and the Bar Z ranch were as inviting as a pit of snakes.

She walked swiftly, staying in the shadows, but she felt vulnerable in the darkness. She stayed parallel to the highway, but feared she might be seen from the road. Even more she feared the wild land on her side of the fence.

Too aware of the noise she was making as she moved through high grass toward the ranch road, she tried to bank her dread about what might come out of the shadows. Her back tingled. She was almost there. As soon as she reached the road, she turned away from the locked gates and the highway. The road had to lead to the ranch house—and to Zach Durham.

As the road curved, trees crowded the border. Her feet made soft thuds, and her heart was pounding so loudly that she barely heard her footfalls. She slowed, almost tiptoeing, her palms damp, while she tried to keep her imagination under control.

The night seemed interminable. When she came out of the forest, she was startled by the brightness of the night. A full moon rose high above her, and she almost groaned aloud. She hadn't given thought to whether it would be a full moon or a new moon. Among the trees, the darkness had been a cover, but in the open, silvery moonlight illuminated the land. Even dressed in a navy long-sleeved T-shirt, jeans and navy sneakers, with her hair tucked under a baseball cap, there would be no hiding beneath the bright beams bathing the earth. With a grim desperation she plunged ahead.

Did the man live at the opposite end of the state? She felt as if she had been walking for hours, yet reason told her it was only a little over an hour since she had pulled her car off the road, locked up, and become a trespasser.

And she worried about the man whose property she was trespassing on. She recalled the comments of the people in the nearby small town of San Luis when she had asked about Zach Durham.

"Zach's a loner."

"He keeps to himself."

"We don't see much of him."

Several men mentioned that they'd seen Zach talking to Amber at a bar in town only a week earlier. That same weekend the police had found Amber's burned, abandoned car, and begun an official search. They'd contacted Emily because her name was found on a slip of paper near the vehicle. The sheriff confirmed what the men had told her: Zach was the last person seen with Amber.

A bird's clear whistle sounded, a high, melodious note that carried on the whisper of wind through the pines. She could detect the damp smell of spruce, and under other circumstances might have been able to enjoy her surroundings, but at the moment they held a foreboding.

Another quarter of an hour passed before she rounded a bend in the road. Ahead, yellow light shone through the trees. Her pulse jumped. She was close to her destination. Now she wished there had been some way to contact him by phone. His number was unlisted, and she hadn't been able to pry it out of anybody in town. Uncertainty struck her.

She intended to look at the house, get a peek at him, see if she could discover any reason for Amber to be so fearful, and ascertain her missing sister's whereabouts. Now in the dead of night, the idea seemed foolish. She wished she had come during broad daylight and confronted him directly. Yet in the light of day when she'd looked at his locked gates and No Trespassing signs, that idea had seemed unsatisfactory.

With a sigh, she moved forward. Now that she was here, she might as well see what she could discover about her reclusive ex-brother-in-law, a man she'd met only once.

She spotted the house tucked among tall spruce and pines and aspen a few yards later. Only two lights shone through windows, both on the ground floor to the rear. Emily wiped her damp palms on her jeans and strode forward. Her heart drummed as she approached the house. It was a tall Victorian structure, forbidding in the night.

She patted the bag she carried, feeling the doggie treats, wondering if treats would hold a ferocious guard dog at bay. Didn't ranchers always have dogs? She might soon know.

She pulled out the bag of treats, ready to toss them, expecting an animal to charge at any moment. Leaving the road, she stayed in the shadows, inching closer to the house. Her heart pounded violently. A twig snapped and she jumped.

Even if Zach Durham was an honest, upstanding citizen, he could shoot her for trespassing, or mistake her for a burglar. If he was not honest and upstanding, the consequences could be worse. But she had to find her sister, and Zach Durham was the last man Amber had mentioned during her frantic phone call. She could remember Amber's warning about him. Emily wanted to see him, see inside his house, see what she could learn.

She had to cross a stretch of yard that was splashed in moonlight and that looked as bright as daylight. Grimly she rushed across it, flattening herself against the wall of the house, her pulse racing. She listened, fully expecting a shot to ring out or guard dogs to come bounding at her, fangs bared.

Edging along the side of the house, she moved toward

the patch where light spilling through the glass illuminated a bright rectangle of ground. Emily reached the window, and turned to peer inside. Even at five-eleven, she had to stand on tiptoe to see anything.

She was looking into an old-fashioned kitchen with glass-fronted cabinets and a round oak table. At the sink stood a bare-chested man in jeans, his back to her. For just a moment she forgot her fear and her mission as she looked at a muscled back that tapered from broad shoulders to a narrow waist and slim hips. Her ex-brother-in-law. The man looked muscular and fit...and dangerous.

She remembered their one brief meeting after Amber's wedding. Amber had called and announced that she was passing through Chicago on her honeymoon, that the newlyweds wanted Emily to join them for dinner.

Emily remembered a handsome, charming man—but when had Amber ever been with a man who wasn't handsome, sexy—a hunk?

Emily edged closer to the window and stared at him.

He had thick brown hair with a slight wave. He turned, and she was riveted by the sight of him. His chest was muscled, with a sprinkling of dark hair. His stomach was flat and trim, his jeans riding low on his slender hips. His rugged angular face had a scar along his jaw.

His gaze swept toward the window.

Recovering her wits, she dropped to the ground, her heart pounding, terrified that he might have spotted her. She leaned back against the house to get her breath and then looked inside again.

He picked up two glasses of water.

"Keeps to himself. Him and his kids. Never see 'em or talk to 'em much." Sheriff Nunez's words echoed clearly in her mind along with his reasons for not forcing his way into Durham's house to search it. The sheriff said he had to have just cause for a warrant to search the place. Well, maybe she could convince the sheriff there *was* just cause for a search.

Emily looked at the tall man holding the glasses of water. Must be for the kids. Her niece and nephew. Curiosity plagued her. She still couldn't believe Amber had had two babies.

Two babies that Amber had walked away from. Emily felt a stab of remorse. Zach Durham had to have a good side. She prayed he did, and was loving to the children. When Amber had called to tell her she had married husband number three, Emily had asked about Zach and the kids.

"Oh, he's a great dad. His life centers around those kids. Mine doesn't. I'm so happy now. I can't wait for you to meet Raimundo." And Amber had gone on to talk about her latest husband. Years ago when they were children, Emily had given up trying to understand her sister.

She peeked through the window again. Zach was walking toward a door to what must be a hallway. Her gaze raked again over his lean form. His profile—a firm jaw, prominent cheekbones—was rugged, the planes of his face craggy.

Then he was gone and she could see only the empty kitchen. Where had he gone?

She slipped around the corner of the house and stepped back to look at it. All the windows were dark beyond the kitchen. She tiptoed along, keeping close to the wall, thankful when she reached the shadows of an oak. Everything in her cried to get away, yet she had to find out if Amber was here.

"Don't move." The voice was deep, commanding and harsh.

Without thinking, she jumped in fright. With a small cry, she spun around.

Something slammed into her. Pain burst in her ribs; she hit the ground and stars danced in front of her eyes. The damp ground was cool beneath her with a faint scent of pine rising from the disturbed needles. As she fell into a patch of moonlight, she looked up. A man straddled her, his fist raised to strike. She was frozen, unable to speak.

His face was in shadow, hers bathed in moonlight. His fist paused, hanging in the air as she looked up at him and saw his dark eyes staring down at her.

When she locked gazes with him, something unexplainable happened. Tension arced between them. She could all but hear the air crackling with electricity as the moment changed. Her heart thudded, but no longer in fear. She became aware of every inch of him that touched her—his thighs pressed against her sides, his hand on her shoulder. His chest was even more impressive up close, the contours of his muscles highlighted by moonlight.

And he seemed caught in the same stunned suspension. His eyes searched hers and he remained immobile.

Even though she felt vulnerable, a flicker of curiosity about him flared to life and built within her. She stared up at him. Maybe it was his primal urge to defend his home and family that terrified her and at the same time drew her to him.

He lowered his hand slowly to splay his fingers on his thigh. Her gaze followed his hand, and she couldn't resist looking at the fly of his jeans, the taut pull of the worn material over his thigh. Her gaze flew back up to meet his fierce scowl. The magic moment that had danced between them like snow crystals was gone.

"Why are you looking in my windows?"

She could hear the rage in his bass voice. "I had car trouble," she said, realizing he must not remember meeting her. "I'm Amber's sister."

His eyes narrowed while he studied her. In one swift movement that revealed how fit he was, he stood and pulled her to her feet. "Come inside," he said, holding her arm and jerking his head toward the door.

Hurrying to keep pace with him, she stretched out her legs. Her ribs ached from his tackling her, and her heart pounded with fear. Her baseball cap was gone and her hair was coming unpinned, locks curling around her face.

They went up the steps and crossed the porch, then he led her into the house. Watching her, he locked the door.

His hand closed around her arm as he drew her into a room and shut that door, too. Despite her consciousness of the man beside her, she took in a room with bookshelves, a large fireplace, a navy leather sofa, Navaho rugs and beamed ceilings.

He turned to her and his fingers wound in her hair. Pins went flying from her scalp as he tilted her head so he could look into her face.

She gazed into brown eyes so dark they were endless pools of blackness, eyes that held fires of rage in their depths. Her heart pounded because there was no mistaking his fury, and he looked capable of violence.

"Let go of me," she said, hoping she sounded calmer than she felt.

Angry and surprised, Zach stared down into wide eyes, framed by a riot of red curls that tumbled down the back of this intruder's neck. With a stirring of memory, he studied her crystal green eyes, straight nose, slightly pointed chin, prominent cheekbones. Besides their long ago meeting, she looked incredibly familiar. Another face flitted to mind—his daughter's. With her tangle of red curls and big green eyes, her freckled nose and little pointed chin, his daughter could belong to this woman.

"You're my ex-brother-in-law," Emily said in a whispery voice, as if desperately emphasizing their relationship. He could see the vein in her throat and knew her pulse was racing. Anger mushroomed in him. He didn't want anything to do with his ex-wife—or her sister.

"Damn it, what kind of game are you playing? What do you want?"

Emily's heart thudded. His dark gaze was intense, and in her peripheral vision she was too aware of his bare chest and broad shoulders, the faint hint of stubble on his jaw. She could detect the scent of aftershave.

And as she stood looking up at him, tension pulled at her again, making her feel as if the air between them crackled. She felt drawn into his midnight eyes, tumbling into a blackness that carried her on a swift current to an unknown destination. He stood too close and he was too bare. Too virile. When his gaze shifted to her mouth, she couldn't get her breath. She was reacting to him as a man—something she didn't want to do and couldn't recall ever having done so intensely before. In her well-ordered life, there were no moments of irrational, unwanted attraction.

"What in the hell were you doing creeping around my house in the dead of night?" His words broke the spell, jolting her and reminding her that she might be in danger. His hand relaxed in her hair, and her head was no longer pulled back, yet she continued to gaze up at him, locked in his compelling stare.

"I'm looking for Amber," she answered, her voice sounding faint and breathless. Amber's men were probably as unpredictable as was Amber. They could run to violence but that had never kept Amber from flirting with them—or even marrying them. Emily wished desperately she were back in Chicago, safe in her own apartment. Yet in spite of her sense of danger, she was intensely aware of Zach as a strong, sexy male.

His hand shifted to her jaw and she noticed the warmth of his fingers. "You could get hurt badly. Didn't you see my No Trespassing signs?"

"Yes," she whispered as he looked at her mouth again. Just a look and her lips tingled and parted. "You were the last person seen with my sister," she said breathlessly, trying to think about something besides his dark eyes and masculine mouth. "Amber was here, in the Red Rocket Bar a week ago Saturday night."

The tenseness left his shoulders, but pinpoints of anger still danced in his eyes.

"Are you carrying a gun?"

"No," she answered.

He inhaled, his broad chest expanding. Then he stepped away. "Why didn't you just call me? We're not complete strangers."

"To all practical purposes, we are. One brief dinner together doesn't constitute family ties. Besides, your number is unlisted. Zach, I need to find my sister, and I was willing to do anything to get the answers."

"I could have shot you for trespassing."

He sounded disgusted and moved away from her, turning to stare at her with his hands on his hips. It was difficult to keep her gaze on his face; his bare chest was impossible to ignore. She realized it must have been a long time since she had seen a man's chest. It had definitely been a long time since she had seen muscles like his.

"I don't know where your sister is. We parted ways a long time ago and haven't kept in touch. She doesn't come to see her children or write to them or call them." The last was said with bitterness and a hint of accusation, as if Emily, too, were guilty of neglecting them.

"She was here and talked to you a week ago."

"She came into the bar while I was there. I didn't know she was in the state. I talked to her, but I didn't leave with her. I didn't even see her leave. We just talked, that's all. And when I asked her if she would see the children, she said she might the next day."

Something thumped above them, and Emily looked up.

"That's my daughter or son."

"*My* niece or nephew."

"Give me a break," he said with unmistakable disgust. "You've never seen them or talked to them or written them."

"I did write when they were born, and Amber never answered. You and Amber divorced when they were babies. You know Amber and I weren't close. She never invited me to see them and neither have you!"

He waved his hand to stop her excuses. Her gaze wavered and flicked down over him. The knees of his jeans were wet and had smudges of damp earth from their encounter outside.

"Where's your car?" he asked.

"Up on the road."

"That was damn foolhardy."

"Amber called me a week ago and she sounded terrified of someone."

"So you decided it was me?" he asked, arching a dark eyebrow, disgust returning to his voice.

"She was in this area—why else would she be here?"

"Your sister is totally unpredictable. I saw her only briefly and she didn't tell me about any plans. And she didn't act afraid of anything. Far from it. She was flirting and having her usual good time."

Zach knew he sounded bitter. Amber was a tall, drop-dead gorgeous blonde and he had fallen for her, marrying her within a month of meeting her. They had married in Las Vegas, spent two nights there, flown to New York and spent a week there. On the way home they had stopped in Chicago and had had dinner with the sister. He barely remembered Emily because at the time he only had eyes for Amber. The honeymoon had lasted until she discovered she was pregnant and then she had thrown a screaming fit, telling him she was getting an abortion. He had talked her out of it. Zach drew a deep breath. Every thought about Amber stung. Anger burned, flickering between fury at himself for being so blind, and rage at Amber for her attitude toward her children.

And he only half believed the sister. He didn't know what she was up to. When Amber had sashayed into the bar last week, she hadn't acted frightened. He remembered her sitting next to him, flirting as her hand played over his thigh. Even though she wore Husband Number Three's wedding ring, Zach knew he could have brought her home to his bed. She would have stayed a while, grown restless again, especially with the children, and gone on her way. He didn't intend to fall into that trap again, or to let her get the children's hopes up—only to disappoint them again.

"Did she tell you anything about another man?" Emily asked, bringing his thoughts back to her.

Zach shook his head, knowing he was being uncooperative. But he had been badly hurt by Amber. And he blamed himself for being such a fool over her and letting his body rule his mind and heart. The woman was shallow and selfish, and he should have seen it clearly.

He didn't want to deal with her sister, either. He wanted to get her out of his house and send her on her way. He wasn't concerned with this woman's problems. Let her search for her sister. Never again did he want to be involved with Amber.

And all the time he was angrily deciding to get rid of her, Emily's big green eyes tugged at him. In spite of the pull, he intended to stay out of it—even though it was obvious she didn't know the first thing about searching for a missing person.

"Did you see her with any other man?"

"She talked to other guys. That's the last I remember."

Feeling defeated and frustrated, Emily stared at Zach. Something didn't seem right about him. He was a rancher, yet he kept to himself. She had always thought ranchers were friendly people. But Zach kept the road to his house fenced and locked.

"I tackled you pretty hard," he said, interrupting her thoughts. "In the dark, I thought you were a man."

"That comes from being almost six feet tall," she remarked dryly.

"Are you all right?"

She nodded, touching ribs that ached badly. "A little sore."

"I'll get the kids, and we'll drive you back to your car. You shouldn't have left it on the highway."

"Don't wake them at this hour. I can walk back."

"No, you can't. I think they're awake, anyway. I'll go see."

"Isn't it late for little children to be awake?"

"They went to bed a long time ago. They woke up and

wanted drinks of water. Since my divorce, they don't sleep well. If they're asleep again, I'll carry them down."

"May I come see them?"

He glanced at her, seeing the uncertainty in her expression. He knew Amber's moods and the chronic liar and actress that she was. He suspected the sister was the same, and wondered if she was trying to soften him up. She couldn't give a damn about the children because she knew nothing about them.

"I suppose." He leveled a look at her that made her draw a shaky breath.

Emily felt anger and dislike radiate from him like heat from a wood stove. "You don't even know me, yet you dislike me."

He had started toward the hall. He stopped and swung around. "I know you're Amber's sister. You're blood kin. Your sister is coldhearted, completely wrapped up in herself. There are two little children upstairs that have been hurt damnably by her."

He left the room and Emily trailed behind him, watching the play of muscles in his back. She was stunned by his anger. She couldn't argue with him. And she suspected that this man had been as badly hurt as the two children.

As she walked beside him into the hall, she was aware of his height. She was nearly six feet tall, yet he was taller than she by a good seven or eight inches.

"Why aren't the police searching for Amber?" he asked as they climbed the stairs.

"They have started searching," she replied. "Last weekend they found her car abandoned and burned."

Zach frowned. "I saw that car on the television news, but it didn't say anything about Amber." And in the numerous times Zach had spoken with Nunez about Amber, the sheriff never once mentioned the burned-out car or that Amber was considered a missing person.

"They found my name on a slip of paper that was in the

grass near the car. They called me before they were absolutely sure it was her car.''

"I can't imagine your sister isn't somewhere doing exactly what she wants. On the other hand, maybe she finally went too far with someone.''

"I'm worried about her. She sounded terrified when she called me.''

He shrugged and continued up the steps in silence. At the top of the stairs, he motioned toward an open door. As they entered, she heard a thumping. Zach switched on another light that revealed a black retriever sprawled on the floor, his tail thumping loudly. The dog got to its feet and crossed the room toward them.

"This is Tiger.''

"I was afraid of a watchdog.''

"Yeah, well, this is one of them—and he's as tough as vanilla pudding.''

She scratched the dog's head and followed Zach across the room to a narrow child's bed that had a play castle as a headboard. He leaned over the bed and Emily reached out to grasp his arm. The instant her fingers closed around his muscled forearm, she felt an acute awareness of him. "Don't wake her,'' she whispered. "I can walk to my car.''

His eyes narrowed as he looked at her hand and then at her.

Emily's gaze ran past him to the child, and she forgot the man.

"Oh, great saints,'' she whispered and moved closer, forgetting Zach Durham's existence as she looked at the hauntingly familiar sleeping child.

Two

Zach stared at Emily. Her face paled and she moved closer, brushing against him as she leaned over the bed. He looked from her to his sleeping baby and he knew why she was stunned. The child looked like her child. Two heads of red ringlets caught the light and reflected gold in their depths. Two pairs of eyes were fringed with thick, auburn lashes. Two straight noses were sprinkled with freckles. And he knew if Rebecca opened her eyes, they would match the green of Emily's.

Amber had been a natural redhead, but she had always kept her hair dyed blond. And it was straight, bearing little resemblance to Rebecca's curls.

Zach watched Emily reach out to touch one of those curls, letting it wind around her finger. He frowned and studied her, remembering the times Amber had played him for a fool with her lying. Did the sister really feel moved by the sight of her niece, or was this some ploy?

She stepped closer, and he wondered whether she was

aware of his existence. As he stared at her, he fought a strange battle with his emotions. He didn't want to soften his feelings toward her. She was Amber's sister! Yet he couldn't help feeling less hostile toward her as she stared at Rebecca. Tears glistened in Emily's eyes, and he watched her swipe her hand across her face.

If she was so moved by the sight of her niece, why hadn't she written or contacted them? Yet already he knew the answer. Amber kept no ties to anyone. He knew almost nothing about Amber's family except that the father was in prison for robbery.

He walked to the center of the room and waited until Emily turned from the bed. Her face was pale and her expression was forlorn as if she had just lost something valuable. He had a ridiculous urge to wrap his arms around her and tell her she could stay and get to know Rebecca.

He shook off the impulse. "You can stay here tonight and we'll take you to your car in the morning," he said, wondering if even this gesture was a sign that he had lost his wits.

"Oh, no! I don't want to put you out. It wasn't that bad a walk. I really don't mind."

"We have plenty of room here," he said, realizing she didn't want to stay any more than he wanted to have her. "Either you stay or I wake them."

She bit her lip as if torn and glanced back at Rebecca. "I'll stay. Please don't wake them. May I see Jason, too?"

"Sure," he answered, realizing there were things she probably wanted to know about her sister—things he didn't want to get into right now.

"Don't turn the light on in his room. The hall light will be enough," she said.

"Nothing except bad dreams will wake them. They can sleep through storms, noise, light." He crossed the hall with her at his side and switched the light on in another small bedroom. Two fuzzy mutts blinked sleepy eyes and wagged their tails.

"The dogs are Tater and Spot."

Barely noticing the small dogs, Emily crossed the room to a narrow, four-poster bed. She leaned over it and looked at the sleeping three year old. The little boy had a mass of brown ringlets, the same freckled nose, the same pointy chin. Again shocked by the unmistakable resemblance, Emily moved closer, lost in thought.

How could Amber have run away and left them behind? Emily glanced over her shoulder at Zach, who lounged in the doorway and watched her. Was he to blame?

Emily felt a pang. She had never expected to have marriage, a husband, or children in her life. God knows, her family genes should not be passed on to another generation. Or so she had always thought—these two little children carried those genes and they looked sweet, innocent and adorable.

How could Amber have left them? The question tore at Emily again. It had to be Zach. No mother would willingly leave such angels—not even Amber, though she had never taken responsibility for anything in her life.

Zach turned and motioned toward the door. Emily tiptoed out while his boot heels scraped the floor with each step.

"The dogs stay up here?"

"They won't leave those kids." He changed the subject. "Let's get something to drink. I have ice tea, coffee, milk or beer."

"Tea's fine," she said, then lapsed into silence. Zach wanted some answers from her and he knew there were things he should tell her. Sheriff Nunez was a close-mouthed, noncommunicative man and must not have said much to her about Amber. Nunez hadn't even told *him* everything the police knew. And the sheriff certainly hadn't mentioned talking to Emily.

Zach switched on the light in the kitchen. As soon as Emily stepped inside, he turned to face her, blocking her path. "Before I get drinks, let's talk."

"Sure," Emily replied, puzzled, wondering whether there was something about Amber she didn't know. Was he going to tell her?

Zach placed his hands against the wall on each side of her, hemming her in, moving in too close. She could feel the warmth of his body, smell his hair. The determination in his eyes made her want to duck and run.

"You said you came looking for your sister. I think you ought to tell me more about it. Amber could be involved in anything with anybody. She wasn't very discriminating. You may be in danger, too. You may have led someone to us and put us both in danger."

Startled by his remarks, Emily frowned. "You're standing too close."

"Yeah, I am. I want some answers from you." His direct gaze disturbed her, and she was again acutely conscious of him. The urge increased to push past him, but there was a forcefulness about him that held her immobile. And something more held her in place; her heart raced with a visceral awareness of his appeal as a male.

"I don't see how I can be in danger or bring any jeopardy to you. No one is interested in me. And if someone is after my sister, I haven't had any contact with her since the one phone call—and no one could know about that." Emily answered in a clipped tone, annoyed that she was responding to him in an elemental way.

Zach gazed down into thickly lashed green eyes that were wide and guileless. He had told himself over and over to stay out of her problems. He didn't need more worries. He had the children's safety to think about. He didn't need to take someone else under his wing. And never would he want to be involved with anyone who had the slightest connection to Amber. Stop questioning her, he scolded himself. Take the woman to her car in the morning, get her to the nearest motel and tell her goodbye.

And maybe he had developed a gut instinct for trouble. Somehow he felt she might jeopardize his life and the children's. If Amber was involved with the wrong people, Emily could place herself in peril by asking questions about her sister. He didn't want any part of the problem. He had no interest in seeing Amber again. He was starting to get his own life together, trying to get some stability into the lives of the kids. The last thing he needed was to bring danger to them. He looked down into innocent eyes and caught a scent of lilacs and spring flowers.

"I have to try to find Amber," she said.

"You could get hurt badly—" he seemed to have a thought "—when did you get here?"

"I took time off work and drove. This afternoon I arrived in San Luis, met with Sheriff Nunez and talked to people in town. Why?"

"I just wanted to know who you've talked to, what you might have stirred up. If someone was following you, you wouldn't know it."

"Why would anyone follow me?"

"You don't know what your sister was involved in."

"No, I don't."

Satisfied with her answers, he moved away and got a pitcher of tea from the fridge. He poured it over ice in a tall glass and handed it to her. "Sugar or lemon?"

"No, thanks," she answered in a subdued voice, watching him warily. He knew she was afraid of him and that suited him fine. He didn't want to get too close to her. Drink a beer and go to bed and get rid of her in the morning, he silently told himself again.

But should he tell her about Jason? It was only a matter of time until she learned the truth.

Zach uncapped the beer, grabbed a chair and sat down facing her. She wasn't the knockout beauty her sister was, but Emily was pretty. And she was sexy. He suspected she didn't realize the latter, but he could feel electricity between them when he got close to her.

Amber had been incredibly sexy, but she had known it and flaunted it. He remembered seeing her last week in the bar in her low-cut, clinging red blouse, dyed blond hair piled high on her head, pouty lips. No man would forget her. Damn few could resist her. Heaven knows, he hadn't been able to. But that was a long time ago.

He took a drink and then lowered the bottle, glancing across the table into Emily's eyes. He was ensnared. She didn't have the faintest idea how to search for her missing sister, and she didn't seem to believe him about the danger.

Leave it alone, he reminded himself. Yet her eyes were focused on him with an intentness that made him uneasy. She might get hurt and that worried him—and it annoyed the hell out of him that it worried him.

"You're not married?"

"No, I'm not."

"Regular guy in your life?"

"No, there's not."

"I find that a little hard to believe."

"I've said it before and I'll say it again—I'm entirely different from my sister. I don't date a lot. I'm very busy with my work."

"Where do you work?" he asked, thinking about what she had just told him. She didn't date, hadn't dated much. In spite of her direct gaze and sincere tone, he didn't believe her. She was too poised, attractive and sexy to spend evenings alone.

"I work for Chicago Charities. It's a privately funded organization that does charity work for families. We provide counseling, handle adoptions, and maintain a home for battered women. We work closely with city agencies."

Zach stared at her, realizing she had been telling the truth when she insisted that she was different from her sister. Amber could never have held a job like the one Emily just described, nor would Amber want to. He began to see Emily in a whole new light. And he realized how dangerous that might be. The last thing on earth he wanted to feel was an attraction to a relative of Amber's. His *ex-sister-in-law*, for Pete's sake!

"Your title?"

"I'm executive director and I oversee the counseling, decide which families we will help, work on the adoptions, check on the women who are in the shelter. The executive committee and I decide how the money will be dispensed when there is a catastrophe and donations come in." She added, "I love my work."

He could imagine her in the kind of job she described. She looked soft, caring. A small light above the sink was the only illumination and it made a halo of her red-gold hair. Locks of it were still pinned to her head, but tendrils had fallen and curled around her face. He imagined all of it free and tumbling loosely over her shoulders.

"What did you do—take a few days off?"

"Yes. I haven't taken a vacation since I started working there, so I have a lot of time coming—more than I plan to take."

She looked much younger than Amber, he found himself thinking. At first he would have guessed Emily's age at about twenty-three, but she had to be older to hold the job she described. He took another drink of beer. Stay out of her problems and get her on her way home, he reminded himself. His gaze swung back to her and worry was plain in her expression as she bit her lip and gazed beyond him.

He needed to avoid her dilemma, to keep to himself— to build a home and a haven. He had a ranch to run. And there was already a crowd. He had the two kids to protect and care for. And there was the retriever he had found near the highway. Plus the two mutts that had been abandoned, and the cat that had appeared from nowhere. He thought about Nessie who stayed with the children. He didn't need to take another living thing under his roof, especially one so desirable.

"There's a possibility your sister is with someone of her own choosing. She didn't act like a frightened woman when I talked to her. Or like a woman on the run." Before Amber had sat down beside him, he had seen her flirting with other men in the bar. "My advice would be to go home and wait a while. She'll call. Believe me, she wasn't frightened that night. Far from it. She was having a good time." He felt like swearing as Emily's dainty chin raised defiantly and her eyes blazed with determination.

"I talked to the bartender at the Red Rocket," she said, "and he gave me a list of names of men who were there that night or who frequent the place. I want to ask them about Amber." She ran her fingers across her forehead. "Do you have aspirin? My head is pounding."

He stood and crossed to a cabinet to get a small bottle and bring it back to her. As she shook out two aspirin and took them, he pulled his chair around the table. "Turn around. I'll massage your neck. Sometimes that works better than aspirin for a headache."

After a momentary hesitation, she turned her back to him.

He spread his legs and moved his chair close behind her, again catching the faint scent of flowers in her perfume. Wisps of red hair curled against her nape as he began to massage her neck. He could feel the tension in her shoulders. Her bones felt delicate and as he kneaded her shoulders, she leaned her head forward and began to relax. Her flesh beneath his hands was warm and soft. He wanted to touch her, and he knew he was playing with fire by doing so. He removed a remaining pin from her hair and the last locks tumbled down.

She turned to slant him a frown over her shoulder. "What are you doing?"

"Relax," he said, amused that she was so bristly. "I'm giving you a massage. You feel better already, don't you?"

She turned around without answering. He worked his hands into her hair, rubbing her scalp, massaging her slender neck. As he stroked her head, he heard a soft murmur from her, and a few minutes later a long, pleased sigh. With every sound of satisfaction she made, he felt his temperature rise. She wiggled slightly beneath his touch, stretching her back.

He worked his hands down her back until she twisted away from him.

"I hurt on my side."

"From my tackle?" he asked, feeling a stab of guilt for being so rough with her.

"Yes," she said, touching the ribs on her right side lightly.

"Does it hurt to take a deep breath?"

"A little."

"Maybe I should take you to an emergency—"

"I'll be fine," she said, her voice becoming softer as his hands moved across her shoulders and neck. "That does feel good. And the aspirin is working."

"Good," he said. She was responding to his massage like a cat being stroked. What would it be like to kiss her? he wondered. The moment the question arose, he closed his mind to speculation. Stay away from the lady, he silently reprimanded. He ought to get up, move and put the table between them. Instead, he continued to massage her slender shoulders even while silently lecturing himself on the dangers of becoming involved.

"Do you have the list of names you got from the bartender?"

Shifting to one side, she pulled a paper out of her jeans hip pocket. He couldn't help noticing the material pulled tautly across her round backside. He took the list she handed to him. Spreading it on the table, he looked at the neat printing. As he went back to massaging her neck, he scanned the page and frowned. "I know a few of these men. Some are trouble. Two are ex-cons. You ought to leave them alone."

"It's the only lead I have to her. Besides you." She moved away and turned her chair, twisting to face him. "You can stop now."

He wanted to keep on touching her. He was so caught

up in kids and day-to-day ranch life that he couldn't recall the last time he'd been alone with an appealing woman. The last time he'd been close to one, touched one. Too damn long and too dangerous to think about now.

"Thanks so much. I feel better," she added.

"Always happy to oblige a lady," he answered lightly.

Her eyes twinkled, and she flashed him a smile. Startled by the change in her, he was dazzled. She had a dimple in her left cheek, and for just a moment worry vanished from her expression. It was like a flash of sunshine on the cloudiest day, and he warmed to it instinctively. "So your opinion of me has improved a notch," she said in a teasing voice.

He couldn't resist leaning closer and looking directly into her eyes. "It's improved enough to scare the hell out of me. Your job is impressive," he added quickly, wanting to change the subject after his blunt, truthful answer to her. "You're here searching for your sister, which is more than she would do if *you* had called *her*." He moved to the other side of the table again, feeling he needed the barrier between them.

"I have to do what I have to do. I haven't ever been able to ignore my family. Someone has to look after them."

He wondered about her because she seemed exactly what she professed to be—a woman entirely different from Amber. Yet there had to be similarities. His thoughts slid to Jason. He needed to tell Emily about Jason, but that was a subject he had never liked to discuss. "Keep in mind that your sister could have left the Red Rocket with some man and be in California or Mexico by now. I still think you ought to go home and leave the search to the lawmen. Or hire a P.I."

"I can't do that. I can't sit idly by. I've always stood by my family. Someone has to."

He felt another clash of wills. Anger pierced him. He reached across the table and retrieved his beer, tilting it to take a drink. He looked at her full lips. She said she didn't date often. What did the woman do—hibernate? Whatever she did, she needed to go home now.

"Don't go see those men."

"I'm not accustomed to taking orders from strangers," Emily replied, annoyed with his dictatorial attitude.

"Maybe you don't like taking orders from anybody. You could easily put yourself in jeopardy. You're out of your element in this part of the country."

"I suppose I am, but I need to get some answers. And that includes questions about you." Emily wondered about Zach and his ranch. Sheriff Nunez said Zach had inherited his ranch, which meant his family had roots in the area that went way back. He was no stranger to the people here, so why the reclusiveness? She thought about the locked gates and barbed wire and chain-link fencing, and about his standoffishness with neighbors.

"Why are you locked in? Isn't that a little unusual for a rancher?"

"It gives me a feeling of security with the kids."

She wondered about his answer—which really wasn't an answer. The man seemed shut in his own world with a high fence around himself. Was he hiding from something—or someone? Emily started to ask him.

A small cry came from the doorway and they turned. Rebecca stood in the door, a tear on her cheek, her eyes sleep-filled and her expression forlorn. She wore pink pajamas with lace trim and teddy bears dancing over them, and her small feet were bare. She held a worn teddy in her arms and pulled a frayed, small blanket behind her. "Daddy?" Her lower lip was thrust out.

"Come here, baby," Zach said softly, and she crossed the room to him.

Her question forgotten, Emily stared at Zach, amazed by the transformation in him. All the harshness about him seemed to fall away. He softened into a gentle, appealing man as he spoke tenderly to the little girl. At that moment he looked completely trustworthy and gentle. And vulnerable. Then he glanced around, and she looked into his dark eyes—and the feeling of danger returned. His shuttered look made her feel that he wanted to be alone.

Emily's gaze went to Rebecca and she was again astounded. She could see a resemblance to her own childhood pictures, a resemblance to herself now. If Rebecca saw any similarity, it was of no significance to her. She glanced briefly at Emily, then went straight to Zach and reached up. He swung her into his lap and she snuggled against him while he cradled her in his arms.

"Did you have a dream?"

She nodded.

"We have company, Rebecca. This is your Aunt Emily. Aunt Emily, this is Rebecca, who is now four years old."

Rebecca looked around and Emily felt the direct, assessing stare of the child.

Emily smiled. "Hi, Rebecca," she said softly.

Rebecca blinked, tightened her lips, and turned her head against Zach, burying her face against his chest. She pulled her blanket up to hold it close.

Zach stroked her hair gently, and Emily was amazed again by the change in him. She was beginning to wonder what had possessed him to marry Amber, but then all she had to do was think about Amber. Men were always dazzled by her. All men. Zach looked as red-blooded as they came.

"Sometimes she has bad dreams," he said quietly, his breath blowing against wisps of Rebecca's red curls.

"What do you do about the children during the day when you work?"

"I hired a woman to help with the kids. She lives in a small house on the ranch. During the week and on Saturday morning she stays until I get home. Vanessa Galban. The kids call her Nessie."

"Then do you take care of them on Saturdays and Sundays?"

"Don't sound so amazed."

Embarrassed, she shrugged and looked down at Rebecca in his arms. "She's asleep."

"She's a restless little sleeper." He raised his head to look at Emily. "I'll take her back to her bed. There's an extra bedroom. You'll have to wait while I make up the bed, but you can have that room."

"Just give me the sheets and I'll make the bed," Emily said. She stood and carried her glass and his bottle to the counter. "I'll get the light."

He shifted Rebecca in his arms and went to check the lock on the back door. He switched on an alarm and then turned to join her.

"You're careful," she said.

"Not careful enough. If I had been on my guard, you wouldn't have gotten so close to the house. I have yard lights, but I stopped bothering to turn them on at night. I'll go back to it, now."

"You're worried about prowlers?"

"You should be more careful," he said, avoiding an answer to her question and coming to stand only inches from her. She could detect the faint smell of beer on his breath. "You don't know what your sister is involved in. I still think you should go home to Chicago in the morning."

"No, I can't."

He shook his head and turned for the hallway. "Come on. I'll put Rebecca in bed and get your sheets." As he started out of the room, Emily picked up the scrap of paper the bartender had given her, then switched off the kitchen light.

Leaving Emily waiting in the upstairs hall, Zach carried Rebecca to bed. Then he returned to remove sheets from a linen closet, and directed her to a bedroom. Switching on the lights, he moved to the four-poster queen-size bed. Emily glanced around a room that held a hodgepodge of furnishings, a bookcase filled with books, a cedar chest, an armoire, a small chest, and a rocker.

"Unfortunately, this is an old house. There are only two

bathrooms here—a small one connecting Becky's and Jason's rooms, and a big bathroom connecting my bedroom and this room. You can lock the doors when you're in it.''

"I'll manage.''

"I'm sure you always do,'' he said quietly, looking down at her. Her head came up. He touched the tip of her nose lightly with his finger. "You look like the capable type.''

"I've had to be. I'll make up the bed.''

"Here,'' he said, flipping back a comforter. "We can both get it made in half the time.'' He snapped a fitted cover over the corner of the bed, while she bent to fit the opposite corner. They worked together efficiently. But she had to make an effort to concentrate on the sheets, and ignore the flex and play of his muscles as he bent and stretched. In minutes the bed was done.

"I'll get you one of my shirts. It ought to make a good enough nightshirt.''

He strode through the bathroom door and in seconds was back to toss a chambray shirt on the bed. "I think I can find a new toothbrush. It might be a child's size because I keep extra for the kids. There's a cabinet in the bathroom with towels and washcloths. Help yourself.'' He crossed the room to face her. "It will be bedlam in the morning when the kids are up. For the last time I'll say it—you should get in your car first thing and go home to Chicago.''

She shook her head.

"Stubborn green eyes,'' he said quietly, looking down at her. She stared at him intently, and he felt as if he were sinking in quicksand. With every word he was getting more involved in her life. "If you *have* to look for her, hire a P.I.''

"I have to do this myself. I can't go home without knowing something, or at least trying my best to find out where she is.''

He shook his head and started toward the bathroom.

"Zach,'' Emily said quietly, her curiosity about him returning. "You live behind locked gates and high fences.

People in town say you keep to yourself. You have an alarm and yard lights. Are you hiding from someone? Is there anyone who would hurt Amber to get at you?''

Zach clamped his lips together and turned back toward her. She felt her insides tighten, felt a premonition of disaster. She almost wished she could take back her question. He looked grim, as if he were holding in check the smoldering anger she had first seen in his eyes.

''Sooner or later, I knew I would have to tell you.''

Three

—

"Jason is not my son."

"What?" Emily stared at him, thinking about the little boy who looked like her own child. "Except for his brown hair, he looks exactly like Rebecca."

"They have the same mother. Your sister had an affair with another man."

"Great saints," Emily said, closing her eyes. She looked at Zach, who gazed at her with impassive eyes. Yet a muscle worked in his jaw and she knew every word hurt him.

"There are rumors in town and I'm sure people know who Jason's father is. But I love Jason. I'm raising him as my son and claiming him as my son."

"That doesn't explain the locked gates."

"Amber had an affair with Stoney Fogg. The Foggs are no-good, worthless, boozing troublemakers. Never big trouble—moonshine, petty theft. They're chronically unemployed, lazy. Old man Fogg and his wife regularly beat each other up. He's a drunkard. When Amber had the affair with Stoney, she and I had already stopped living together as man and wife. She was bored. If she hadn't gotten pregnant, she would have left me sooner.''

Zach raked his fingers through his hair, the strands springing back and some locks falling across his forehead. "She and Stoney had a wild, rocky relationship. When he learned she was pregnant, he didn't want any part of the baby and left town. Later, after Jason was over a year old, Stoney came back and he and Amber ran away.''

Emily gave a small cry and rubbed a hand across her eyes. Zach was startled. He frowned, wondering whether she was acting for his benefit.

"You should know your sister by now—and not be surprised,'' he snapped.

Her head came up. "She's so casual about what I hold sacred. I'll never have children and it hurts to hear about Amber's coldness toward her own.'' She drew herself up. "Go on. I interrupted you.''

"I divorced her,'' he answered, only half thinking about what he was saying. Emily had said she could never have children. He wondered why. "Later Stoney came home without Amber. She never married him, and I heard she married someone in Mexico.''

"She did. This past year she called and said she was Mrs. Raimundo Morales.''

"Yeah, well, last year, Stoney decided he wanted his son. I don't think he wanted Jason as much as he wanted to aggravate me. Stoney and I have crossed paths before, and I once caught him with Amber. We fought and I took Amber home.''

Emily sat on the rocker. She suspected Zach's statement "I took Amber home'' covered the fact that he'd whipped Stoney Fogg badly.

How could Amber have been so irresponsible? Yet Emily knew the answer to her own question. Amber had always been irresponsible. Emily hurt for Zach. He was impassive; his voice was devoid of emotion, which was even more of an indication that he was fighting his hurt over Jason. And probably his hurt over Amber. He must still be terribly in love with her, in spite of his anger.

"I told Stoney he would never have Jason. No court in the country would allow it and he knows it. But knowing him, he wouldn't try through the legal system. All he knows is to steal what he wants."

"Then the fences and alarms are to keep him from getting Jason?"

"Yes. I work all over this ranch and I worry about that thug getting on the property and taking Jason. He might take Rebecca, too, just because she's there. Stoney doesn't think rationally."

"Is Stoney angry with Amber? Would he harm her?"

"I've thought about that," Zach said, rubbing his neck and moving restlessly. "He's unpredictable and wild, but none of the Foggs have ever really done any serious harm to anyone. Something could happen that he didn't intend, but if Stoney did something to Amber, I think he would run. When he's gotten into trouble, he's always fled."

"Do you know if he's still around here?"

"No, I don't, but that will be easy to check tomorrow. Since he hangs out in bars, I can find out."

"Do you feel the children are safe from him during the day when you work?"

"Yes. Nessie is a pit bull. She'll protect them, and I have the alarms. Every man who works for me knows to watch for Stoney. I always wear a pager when I work, and I have a phone in my pickup."

Silence stretched between them while Emily thought about all he had told her. "Zach, how do the children get along? Do they miss their mother terribly?"

"No, they don't. Rebecca remembers her the most. But Amber never was a mother for them. Not from the first moment. She didn't want to have either one of them. She thought she was protected. She had surgery after Jason to make absolutely certain she'd never have another baby."

Emily flinched, hating Amber's rejection of her children, thinking how foolishly Amber had tossed away two precious children and a man who loved her. "I've never understood my sister."

"Yeah, well, that's all the more reason to go back to Chicago tomorrow." Abruptly, he walked toward the bathroom, obviously having talked all he wanted to on the subject of Stoney Fogg. "You can have the bathroom first. Towels are in the cabinet and I'll leave you a new toothbrush. Open the bathroom door on my side when you're out."

"Thanks."

He left, and she heard the door to his bedroom close behind him. She went to the large bathroom, and looked at his green towel hung carelessly on a rack. His razor and shaving cream were laid out near the sink. A new purple toothbrush, still in the package, was propped beside lotion bottles. She turned the lock on the door and peeled off her clothes, stepping into the footed tub and pulling a shower curtain around it. But all the while her mind was on what he had told her. Where was Amber and what kind of trouble had she gotten into this time?

Removing his boots, Zach felt the tension knot his stomach. He hated having old memories of Amber dredged up. Would the woman ever be completely out of his life? Emily was a surprise, though. She was so unlike her irresponsible sister and father. He clenched his jaw. But she was bound to be like them in some ways, and even a little would be intolerable. In the morning he would get her to her car, and then forget her *and* Amber. He was certainly not going to help her search for Amber. He would find out if Stoney was around, and check out the list from the bartender, but that was all. Nothing more. Then he would send Emily Stockton on her way.

When water splashed in the tub, he glanced at the closed bathroom door without seeing it, his thoughts going beyond the door to the shower. Erotic images danced in his mind of Emily beneath the silvery spray of water, and his imagination ran wild. Her skin was rosy and beautiful, her waist tiny. The navy T-shirt had clung to inviting curves and the jeans had revealed long legs. He had no trouble imagining her without the clothes.

Annoyed with himself, he growled and moved across the room. Impatiently, he emptied his pockets and tossed keys and coins on a mahogany chest of drawers, trying to stop thinking about Emily—and failing. Her remark about not having children floated in his mind. She couldn't have a baby. Could that be part of why she didn't date much?

He glared at the bathroom door, hands on hips, and voiced his mission aloud. "Get up in the morning and take her to her car and forget her." He looked at himself in the mirror. "Did you get that, Durham? The lady is stubborn and does what she wants. She's of age and she's got the same blood in her veins as your ex. Don't get involved." He gave a firm nod and walked to the window to turn the shutters and look outside. Lights shone over the grounds and on the hard-packed dusty drive.

Who had burned Amber's car? What was Amber involved in? And could searching for her sister put Emily in danger?

He glanced at the bathroom door again. The water had stopped running and he could imagine Emily toweling dry. He groaned as his body responded to his thoughts. "Go home, Emily Stockton. Get out of my life."

Emily pulled on the chambray shirt that smelled freshly laundered. It was worn, with little threads showing along the frayed collar. Her skin tingled as she thought about the shirt's owner and remembered his hands moving on her shoulders and neck, giving her the firm massage that had helped extinguish her headache. He was a very appealing man. And he might be right about Amber. But danger or not, she had to try to find her sister.

She brushed her teeth, gathered her things and unlocked the bathroom door. When she opened it, Zach turned to face her. He stood barechested and barefooted, the top button of his jeans unfastened. Surprised to find him only yards away, she stared at him, wondering whether he had been waiting to get into the bathroom. His gaze drifted down over her and back up again, and she felt her body tingle as if in that slow assessment he had run his hands over her.

Zach knew he was staring, but he couldn't stop. Her hair was a curly halo around her head. The shirt hid her figure, but it ended mid-thigh and revealed long, long shapely legs. His body tightened and responded, just looking at her. He drew a deep breath and met her wide-eyed gaze. Against all better judgment, he was drawn to her. He moved slowly closer. "My shirt never looked so good."

"Thank you, I suppose," she said as if she couldn't get her breath. She didn't take her eyes from his as she waved her hand. "You can have the bathroom now."

Emily's pulse drummed when he came closer. He stopped only inches away and reached out to touch her hair. "I can't believe you don't date."

"I have a demanding job that I love," she said.

He shook his head. "There has to be more to it than that. Sour love affair, someone hurt you, something...."

She bit her lip as she stared at him. "My sister hasn't been an example to copy," she said, and saw a flicker in the depths of his eyes. Had she hurt him with her blunt answer? "I can't imagine passing on the genes that I carry."

"That's the reason?" he asked with arched eyebrows. "I thought you meant there was a physical problem."

"No. My family life isn't the best. I'm afraid of passing on their mistakes. I'm afraid of becoming like them. My family is worse than the Foggs you told me about. My father is in prison." She was barely aware of what she was saying. She could feel the tension crackle between them. Then Zach's gaze lowered to her mouth and her breathing stopped. She wanted to lean toward him, close her eyes, and let him kiss her. Yet, she knew that was foolhardy in the extreme. All she had to do was remember that he was her ex-brother-in-law.

"That's no reason for you to avoid dating or marriage or having children," he said roughly. "My children carry those same genes and they're good kids."

"I hope and pray they are," she answered, suddenly sorry if she was hurting his feelings. "But I've had a lifetime of seeing nothing but disaster in my family." Tension reigned between them, along with an undercurrent of dangerous attraction, and Emily knew she needed to get away.

"Good night," she said quickly, turning and almost running, closing the door on her side of the bathroom and leaning against it.

"Emily?"

His voice startled her. He was only inches away on the other side of the door. She jumped and then turned to stare at the door. "Yes?"

"What time do you want me to call you in the morning?"

"Whenever you get up."

"Since it's almost half-past four now, I'll sleep in until six."

"Then call me at six."

"Good night."

She tried to busy herself, listening as the water turned on. She could imagine Zach in the shower, remembering clearly how his bare chest and back looked. In minutes, the water stopped. Soon the door opened slightly, and she heard the other bathroom door close as he went to his bedroom.

She sighed and stared into the darkness. Zach said she might be in danger if she kept searching for Amber. Should she do as he urged, and go home? She knew Amber was unreliable, flighty, and could easily be off with some man now, forgetting any danger she might put Emily in. But on the phone Amber had begged for help and had sounded sincerely terrified of a man.

Emily knew she couldn't go home and forget about her

sister. If she did nothing, and something happened to Amber, Emily knew she would never forgive herself.

Where was Amber? Was she still in the area? Emily wondered. She closed her eyes and, in minutes, was asleep.

Some time later, a faint, persistent whine woke her. She opened her eyes to stare into the darkness, momentarily disoriented. Then she remembered where she was, and realized she was definitely hearing a strange, repetitive noise—a high little whine. She turned in bed and looked into a pair of wide eyes.

Emily sat up abruptly, yelped when pain shot through her ribs, and looked down into a small face turned up to her. The little girl kept whining.

"Rebecca?"

The child nodded, and Emily bit her lip, glancing over her shoulder toward the bathroom. She wondered whether to wake Zach or just take the child back to bed.

A small hand reached up and patted the mattress, and Emily's heart melted. She tossed back the sheet. "Do you want to get in bed with me?"

When Rebecca nodded solemnly, Emily reached down to lift the little girl into bed beside her, twisting to protect her aching ribs. Rebecca sniffled, snuggled against Emily and closed her eyes. In seconds she was asleep. Emily pushed a mass of ringlets from Rebecca's face and felt pain grip her heart. Rebecca's hair was like her own hair. Rebecca was like her own child—the one she never expected to have. How could Amber have given up these children? she asked herself again. And Jason wasn't even Zach's son. Yet she suspected as far as Zach was concerned, Jason was his as completely as was Rebecca. From the little she had seen of him tonight, Zach Durham was not what she had imagined he would be.

Emily shut out her thoughts on that subject. She placed an arm across the child and closed her eyes.

When morning came, Zach rolled out of bed and tiptoed to the bathroom, trying to be quiet. As soon as he was dressed in a short-sleeved blue chambray shirt and jeans, he walked down the hall. He carried his boots to put on downstairs so he wouldn't wake anyone.

He opened Jason's door and looked at the sleeping child while the dogs dashed past him and down the stairs. In front of Rebecca's door, Tiger stood wagging his tail. Zach raised his eyebrow.

"Go on, get! I'll let you three outside as soon as I look in on my baby doll."

Tiger turned and disappeared down the stairs as if he had understood every word Zach said. Zach stepped into Rebecca's room, looked at the empty bed and felt a shock. He glanced around the room, wondering if Rebecca had gone downstairs—something she never did. If she awakened, she usually got into his bed. He tiptoed past Emily's door, noticing it was slightly ajar. He was halfway down the stairs before he wondered why.

He set down his boots and went back upstairs to push the bedroom door wider. Aware of the creak of the floorboards, he tiptoed into the room and looked at two heads of red curls. His pulse jumped as he took in Emily's outflung arm. The sheet had been kicked away and she lay on her side, her knees drawn up slightly, her long legs bare. She looked warm, tousled and tempting.

As he stared at her, she opened her eyes and gazed back at him. Her eyes widened and she raised slightly. She grabbed the sheet and yanked it over her legs, her face turning pink.

"I was looking for Rebecca," he whispered, knowing he had been standing there long minutes after discovering them.

"She came in here and wanted in my bed."

"I don't know how she found you, and she usually doesn't take to strangers. I'm sorry if I woke you." He crossed the room. "I'll take her back to bed."

"Don't wake her. I'm getting up now, anyway."

He paused beside the bed. "Sure?"

She nodded, and he didn't want to move away. She looked sleepy, sexy, warm—like a puddle of sunshine that had fallen into his house. "I can't say I blame her. If I could crawl into that bed, I would, too. I'll fix breakfast."

Emily's heart missed a beat at his statement, even though she knew he was teasing. Then he turned and was gone, and Emily stared as the door closed behind him.

She slipped out of bed and tiptoed to get her clothes, the same ones she had worn the night before. With care, she brushed her hair, trying to catch wayward curls. She looped and pinned it on top of her head. Ten minutes later she entered the kitchen.

Zach poured orange juice and turned to hand her a glass. Bacon was cooking in a skillet. "Good morning again. How was the night—except for Rebecca joining you?"

"It was short. I'm sleepy."

"You can go back to bed," he said.

"Of course not." Then, to change the subject, she said, "You're cooking bacon—that's not good for your cholesterol."

"I just cook it on rare occasions—holidays, once or twice a year."

"This is a rare occasion?"

"Yes. I don't have many houseguests," he said. "After we eat and Nessie gets here, I'll take you to your car. Where are you staying?"

"I have a room at the hotel in San Luis."

"That's no place for you!"

"I'll only be there to sleep."

"The San Luis Hotel is above a rowdy bar. It's a fleabag and not safe at night. No tourist or traveler stays in it." Zach couldn't believe Nunez or someone in town hadn't warned her about the hotel.

"Sheriff Nunez said it's all San Luis has."

"That's for damn sure. San Luis isn't on the Interstate and they don't get tourists. We'll bring your car back and

you can stay here. I'll help you look for Amber today."
Zach couldn't believe the words coming out of his mouth.
He had lost his wits, and gazing into her big green eyes
right now wasn't helping.

"Thank you, but I don't want to impose," she answered
primly.

"Yeah, well, you wouldn't be able to stay in that hotel
more than an hour. If you stay there, the locals will think
you're a new hooker. Didn't Nunez tell you not to stay
there?"

"Yes, he did, but that's the only hotel in town. No one
who looks at me will think I'm a hooker. Men won't look
twice."

Her cheeks flushed, and he couldn't resist telling her the
truth. He moved closer and tilted her chin up with his fore-
finger. "Where in hell did you get a notion like that?"

"You think I look like a hooker?"

"Hell, no. But you look sexy and desirable and that's
all that's necessary for the bar crowd. And the hotel is a
place where hookers do business." Her face flushed, and
she looked flustered and uncertain. He wondered about her
past. The woman was from a cosmopolitan city. She probably had a college education and graduate degrees. Yet she
acted like a fifteen-year-old country girl about her looks.
And then he thought about her sister, who was stunning.
Maybe Emily had grown up making comparisons.

"I guess I should say thank-you again," she said, her
voice sounding breathless.

He was tempted to lean down, place his mouth on hers
and taste those lips that should be kissed. Instead, he reminded himself that she was his ex-sister-in-law.

"I think I should stay in town, Zach. I'll be all right, but
thanks for your offer."

He shook his head. "Stubborn woman."

He turned away and moved to the stove to flip the bacon.
"Do you like toast or cereal?"

"Toast is fine," she said. He was reaching to get bread

and put slices in the toaster when a cry erupted from the hall. Jason Durham burst into the kitchen, chasing a large ball.

"Good morning, sunshine," Zach said, gathering Jason into his arms.

"Sunshine!" Jason giggled as he looked at Emily with large, thickly lashed green eyes.

"We have a guest. Jason, this is your Aunt Emily Stockton. Aunt Emily, meet Jason."

"Hello, Jason," Emily said in a friendly tone, as the child stared solemnly at her.

"Shyness has set in," Zach said. "Pray it lasts through breakfast." He set Jason on his feet. "Let's go change you, and then I've got your orange juice and milk. And your cereal." They left and a few minutes later returned, the little boy tagging along behind Zach.

Jason climbed onto a chair and Zach scooted him close to the table, placing breakfast in front of him. As he pushed Jason's red pajama sleeves up, Jason knocked over the glass of milk. As Zach grabbed up the glass and went for a towel, the bacon began to smoke.

"I want my milk!" Jason cried.

"I'll get the bacon," Emily said, turning off the burner and scooping up the slices of bacon, while Zach cleaned the table, poured another glass of milk and quieted Jason.

Emily heard a small cry from the doorway. Rebecca stood with a tiny blanket in hand and her thumb in her mouth. Zach crossed the room to pick her up.

"'Becca, 'Becca!" Jason began to shriek, pounding his spoon on the table.

"Hey, kiddo, cool it," Zach said lightly, taking the spoon and placing it in Jason's bowl. Jason promptly returned to slurping his cereal.

"Good morning, sweetie," Zach said quietly to Rebecca. "How's my girl? Are you having trouble waking up?" She nodded and snuggled against him, her green eyes going to Emily.

"You slept in Aunt Emily's bed."

Rebecca nodded.

"You should have come to my room if you couldn't sleep. Aunt Emily is a guest."

"But I didn't mind," Emily said.

"Drink, Daddy," Rebecca said sleepily.

"All right." He looked down at Rebecca with such tenderness that Emily warmed as if he had been looking at her. "You sit here in your chair. I have your breakfast all ready."

His voice was gentle and he held Rebecca while he got a jar of jam out of the refrigerator.

"I want more milk!" Jason exclaimed, dropping a bite of cereal on the floor.

Emily crossed the room. "Sit down with her and let me get breakfast. I'll get Jason's milk."

Jason reached across the table to take Rebecca's cup of milk, and Rebecca screeched. Zach reclaimed the milk and returned it to Rebecca. He remained calm, his voice quiet and firm, and in minutes—with Emily helping—all four of them were seated at the table.

"You do this pretty well," he remarked as she sipped orange juice.

"I've dealt with kids in my work sometimes," she answered lightly.

Halfway through breakfast, Rebecca fully awakened and began jabbering. As soon as she finished eating, she moved to Emily's side and leaned against her.

"Do you have a little girl?"

"No, I don't have a little girl or a little boy."

"Are you gonna live here?"

"No, I'm not. I'm leaving this morning," Emily answered.

"Rebecca, stop badgering our guest with questions. As soon as you finish breakfast, you're both excused from the table."

Jason climbed down from his chair.

"Remember to brush your teeth. Jason, I'll come help you brush yours."

They both fled the kitchen, and, moments later, Emily heard the television come on in another part of the house.

"Zach, you're very good with them," she said, mildly surprised at how gentle and patient he was with the children, and thinking he had several facets to his personality.

"I feel damned inadequate sometimes," he said as he carried dishes to the sink. "Want anything else to eat?"

"Heavens, no! I'll help you clean," she said, rising from the table and gathering dishes. He turned to take the dishes from her hands.

"None of that. It isn't necessary." He glanced at his watch. "In another ten minutes Nessie will arrive and take charge of this household. I'll take you to get your car. Are your things in your hotel room?"

"No, my suitcase is still in the car. I really think I should stay in town at the hotel. If I need someone, I can call the sheriff and he's only a block away."

Zach turned and picked up the phone, thumbing through a thin phone directory. He punched numbers, and before she knew it Emily was astounded to hear him cancel her room. "She'll be in this morning to pay for last night."

He replaced the receiver. "We'll go get your car. You bring your car back here and ride into town with me. You check out of your hotel room and wait at one of the restaurants while I see what I can find out about Stoney. I'll give Nunez the list from the bar and let him talk to those men."

Emily stared at him and placed her hands on her hips. She tried to control her temper, knowing his high-handed methods were meant to be helpful.

Giving her a long, assessing look, Zach leaned against the counter to face her. "Go ahead. Blow off steam."

"Do you always take charge of people's lives?"

"No, I usually try to avoid that," he answered calmly.

"You're not avoiding it now!" His calm made her temper rise another notch. "You had no right to cancel my hotel room."

"You wouldn't make it through one night."

"Maybe not, but I think I should make that decision. What gives you the authority to take over my life?"

He straightened and Emily watched the subtle transformation—darkened brown eyes, a solemn set to his mouth. She was facing the tough, angry man she had first encountered. A shuttered look crossed his features, and she felt a touch of ice run down her spine. The dark, dangerous stranger had resurfaced, and she felt like backing away. He was formidable to face but knowing he wouldn't physically hurt her, she held her ground.

"You're a stubborn little idiot for trying to find your sister when you don't know how to go about it. You could be in danger now and you're a complete innocent at this sort of thing."

"I suppose you're not!" The moment she said the words, she knew he wasn't. The realization was as much instinctive, as it was based on the way he reacted to danger.

The ring of the phone interrupted their conversation, and Zach stretched his arm out past her to pick up the receiver. She moved away, listening to him talk in monosyllables. Barely aware of his conversation, she was lost in thought about staying at the ranch. Everything in her cried out caution about getting involved with her ex-brother-in-law. And how much could she believe him? How much did she really know about this man?

When she saw him with the children, he seemed kind, trustworthy, capable, intelligent. But when she thought about him in any other way—Amber's ex-husband, the man who had tackled her in the dark last night—she was uncertain and chilled by the toughness in him. And his story about Stoney Fogg—there was no way for her to find out whether Zach was telling the truth or not. Was she being too gullible in believing everything Zach told her?

"She's here."

The words caught her attention. She glanced at Zach to find him watching her, and suddenly realized the phone call must involve her.

"She'll be staying here. I told her I would help her search for her sister." There was a pause, and she saw his jaw tighten and his eyes darken in anger.

"Yeah, I know. Sure thing. Yeah, I'll be in—" he paused and looked at his watch "—about two hours from now. Okay."

He replaced the receiver and shook his head. "Damn sheriff." He crossed the room to her, moving too close. Her pulse fluttered, and she tried to ignore the physical reaction she had to Zach.

"Nunez wants to ask me some more questions about Amber."

Chilled, she gazed up at him. "Have you told me the truth?"

"Yes, but if I hadn't, your question wouldn't give you a good answer."

"I suppose that call is the result of my visit," she said. "I felt he should be questioning you more, maybe come out here and look around."

"So you *did* when he *wouldn't*. Now are you satisfied?"

"I believe you," she answered solemnly, wondering again whether she was being gullible. "Do you want me to go with you to his office?"

"You'll go along and hold my hand as a vote of confidence?"

Startled, she frowned. "Holding your hand would be overdoing it a bit," she answered, and then saw the twinkle in his eyes. "You were kidding me."

"A little. I'll go to his office and answer his questions. He's just covering himself since you're here and raising a fuss. He wants to get reelected." Zach moved close to place his hand on her shoulder. "Nunez can handle the search for your sister. They have an APB out for her. Cops all

over will be looking for her. Go back to your safe world
and leave this up to the police.''

''Would you turn your back if it were your brother—or
your child?''

He sighed, shook his head and placed his hands on his
hips. He looked mildly annoyed, a frown creasing his brow.
''Are you going to be stubborn and foolish about this?''

''No more than you,'' she answered. She felt as angry
as he looked. Most of her life she had made decisions for
everyone around her. She always had for her family, and
now she did so at work. She always had a department of
people working for her but she was unaccustomed to high-
handed methods such as his. As a rancher he was in charge
of his place and everything on it. As long as she stayed
with him, she realized, the clashes would keep coming. Yet
she needed his help. She knew he was right about her lack
of experience at this sort of thing. It was nil. And she hadn't
forgotten her terror as she crept across his land last night
and was tackled by him.

He held out his hand. ''Give me that list of names. The
person who needs to question those men is Nunez.''

She debated whether she wanted to give up talking to
them herself, then decided she would be better off doing
so. She pulled the list from her pocket and handed it to
Zach.

The latch turned in the door and it swung open. The dogs
rushed inside and Emily turned to face a beautiful, petite,
dark-skinned, black-haired woman who looked about nine-
teen years old. She entered behind the dogs, closed the
door, and leaned against it. ''Good morning, Zach.''

Four

Startled, Emily stared at her and wondered if this was the new woman in his life.

"Hi. Nessie, this is Emily Stockton. Emily, meet Vanessa Galban who stays with my kids."

"It's nice to meet you," Nessie said, staring so intently that Emily felt uncomfortable. Nessie's wide dark eyes were thickly fringed with lashes, and she pursed her full lips as she studied Emily. "You must be related," she said, sounding surprised. "The kids look like you."

"Emily is Amber's sister," Zach explained. Nessie frowned, and Emily felt a chilly withdrawal as the woman's gaze swung to Zach.

"Where are the urchins?" she asked affectionately.

"Hear the television?"

"I'll go say hello. Any instructions before I do?"

"Yes."

Emily barely heard their conversation. She stared at a woman who was only a couple of inches over five feet and had flawless skin and silky, black hair. This was the nanny? Did Zach date her? Emily would be amazed if he didn't. She glanced at Nessie's fingers and saw there was no wedding or engagement ring.

Quietly Nessie left the room, and Zach glanced at Emily.

"She's the pit bull?" Emily asked.

He shrugged. "Looks arc deceiving. You should know that from Amber. If she wants to, your sister can look like an angel. Nessie would fight to her last breath for those kids."

"Maybe so, but fighting for them and really protecting them are two different things. She's barely five feet tall."

"She knows where my gun is and how to use it. She practices regularly. Nessie isn't as delicate as she looks. So, how soon will you be ready to go?"

"Give me five minutes," Emily replied, and left for her room, going to the bathroom to brush her teeth. She stared into the mirror, lost in thoughts about Nessie. Zach had to be dating her, she thought. Nessie was gorgeous. "So what if he is?" she asked her reflection. She shouldn't care one whit. But it gave her a tight feeling inside and she knew she did not like the idea. On top of the dislike, she was annoyed with herself for caring. She should not care what Zach Durham did with his life—not at all. Then why did she feel tied in knots since Nessie's arrival? She returned to the kitchen to find Nessie drying her hands and starting the dishwasher.

"You cleaned the breakfast mess quickly."

"There wasn't that much," Nessie answered quietly with a glance over her shoulder at Emily. Emily felt a definite sense of disapproval and wondered whether it was because of Amber or because Nessie didn't want another woman around Zach.

"I'm from Chicago. I'm here because my sister has disappeared."

Turning to face her, Nessie raised an eyebrow. "Did you think Zach would know where she is?" she asked coolly.

"I thought he might. The last time anyone can recall seeing her was the night she was seen talking to Zach at a bar in town."

"He told me he saw her, but he said he didn't leave the bar with her. I was here early the next morning and she was nowhere around here. And he doesn't lie," she added emphatically.

"So I've been told."

Nessie's blue eyes sparked with fire. "Do you think he might have hurt your sister?"

"I don't know what happened to her. The sheriff called me when they found her car burned on the highway."

"No matter what he felt about her, Zach would never hurt her," Nessie said so forcefully that Emily was taken aback. The woman had to be in love with him, and Emily wondered if she had intruded where she was definitely not wanted.

"Listen, Zach may have his problems, but he's one of the best men I've ever known," Nessie declared. "He's saved my life and helped me out. He's wonderful with his kids. He takes in every stray he finds. Ask Quint, his foreman, about him. Or ask any of the guys that work here. Half of them needed a hand up and he gave them one."

"I'm just trying to find out what's happened to Amber," Emily added swiftly.

"Your sister is doing whatever she damn well pleases."

"She called me for help. Look, I have no intention of interfering in any way with you and Zach."

Nessie's eyes grew round and then she shook her head. "Hey. You're jumping to the wrong conclusions. There's no 'me and Zach.'"

Embarrassed, Emily waved her hand. "Whatever you say."

"I feel strongly about him. I love him like a brother. He's taken care of me. He's helped pay my medical bills and he's helping with my tuition. I take care of his kids for him while he works. But that's all there is between us."

"It doesn't matter what's between you," Emily said stiffly, wondering how the conversation had gotten so personal.

"Speak of the devil," Nessie said, her gaze fixed beyond Emily. Zach stood in the doorway and Emily wondered how much of the conversation he had overheard. Embarrassed again, she headed for the kitchen door and stood waiting for him.

"I'm ready."

"I have to tell the kids goodbye and then I'll be there." When he returned, both children trailed after him. He crossed the room to write in a notebook. "Here's where you can get me, Nessie. I'm wearing my pager. Turn on the alarm when we leave, and I've told Quint to tell the others to be on the alert."

"We'll be careful. Don't worry," Nessie said, smiling up at him. Emily looked at the two of them together and couldn't imagine that they didn't date.

"'Bye, Daddy," Rebecca said, holding up her arms. He picked her up and gave her a kiss and hug, while Jason ran in circles around him.

"'Bye, Daddy," echoed Jason, waving his hands and making humming noises as he ran.

Zach set Rebecca down and caught Jason in a hug, making the little boy laugh. Rebecca looked shyly at Emily then walked over to place her thin arms around Emily's legs.

Emily knelt and picked the child up, feeling as if her heart had turned inside out. She smiled at Rebecca. "'Bye, Rebecca. We won't be gone long." Emily set the little girl on her feet, then straightened to find Nessie staring at her intently. She wondered what was on the woman's mind.

"Goodbye, Nessie," she said quietly.

"Goodbye, Miss Stockton."

"Please, just Emily." Nessie nodded, and Emily went outside where the cool morning air held the faint scent of pine.

Moments later, with a broad-brimmed black Stetson

squarely on his head, Zach strode outside, took her arm and they crossed the yard to the pickup. She climbed into the large cab and noticed the two car seats buckled into the back seat for the children.

They drove away from the house, and Emily looked at the land that had been so threatening in the dark and that now looked idyllic and beautiful. Sunlight splashed over the aspen and spruce, birds trilled, and the grass sparkled with dew. Meadows sprawled across a valley that was nestled beneath tall mountains covered in trees.

"Nessie's very beautiful," Emily said quietly.

"I suppose she is."

"Suppose?" She laughed, and he grinned with a flash of white teeth that radiated such charm it made her breath catch.

"We don't date," he said.

"I can't imagine why you wouldn't. She's beautiful."

His smile vanished as his jaw set. "Your sister tore my heart to shreds and then stomped on it. In a lot of ways, it was my own dumb fault. I should have seen what was coming. Now I'm numb. Even though it's lonely as hell, I don't want another relationship. And Nessie has had about the same experience."

Emily heard the pain in his voice and wondered about his solitary life.

"Nessie doesn't approve of me," she ventured.

His head jerked around and he looked at her with narrowed eyes. "It's because of Amber."

"It's not the first time someone has reacted that way to me because of my sister. I don't believe you liked me too well last night for the same reason." Then she asked, "Nessie's no longer married?"

"No."

"I predict you two will date before long."

"No, we won't. We've both been hurt too much to get over it quickly."

"Has she been divorced long?"

"It was final just last month, as a matter of fact." He continued, "One night I was returning to the ranch and found her body on the side of the road. The bastard she was married to had beaten her up and tossed her out of his pickup. I took her to the hospital."

"No wonder she's grateful to you."

"She married young. He abused her and she put up with it since she had been abused as a child. There aren't any shelters out here or any counselors." He glanced at Emily. "She could have used your help at the time."

"Did she leave her husband then?"

"Yes. I suppose Doc Benson and I became substitute counselors. I talked her into pressing charges on the bastard she was married to. She took him to court and he only got probation, but he'll think twice before he beats up the next woman. She got a divorce. I told her I needed a nanny. I taught her to use my pistol and convinced her she could get her GED and go on to get a college degree. She's twenty-one and getting her life in order. She's taking courses by correspondence and she drives twice a week to Santa Fe to take night classes."

"That's wonderful. That's all the more reason I'd think she would be wildly in love with you."

"She's not wildly in love with anyone. When I found her, she had no self-esteem, but she's gradually developing into her own person. I promise you," he stated emphatically, "I don't want to go into another relationship and cause my kids more emotional upheaval. I don't want more disruption myself. No, Nessie and I are friends. She's great with the kids and I'm glad to help her. Besides, she's so young."

"And you're so old."

"I'm thirty-four, but sometimes I feel a hundred."

"Sure. I noticed how tottering you were last night when you tackled me."

He grinned, the tension easing out of him. "That's what you get for sneaking up on me in the dark." He slowed the truck as the main entrance came into view. "I have to unlock the gates."

Zach braked and hopped out of the pickup. Emily watched his long-legged stride as he went around the truck to the gate. In moments he swung it open and returned to the cab.

"When we reach the highway, which way do I turn?"

"West."

"I'm impressed!" With a flash of white teeth he smiled at her. "The city girl knows her directions."

"I'm the member of my family who *doesn't* get lost." She watched as he braked, then accelerated and turned onto the highway. "You're not locking your gate?"

"You can't be too far away. We'll bring your car back to the ranch. It'll be okay for a while to leave the gate open. Nessie is a crack shot and she wouldn't hesitate to stop an intruder. She said she would just imagine it's her ex-husband."

"She said you paid her medical bills and you help with her tuition."

"It's not that much to help someone get back on her feet."

"We could use you at Chicago Charities."

"I'd last about two minutes in the Windy City. I need to be out here where I have some space."

"You don't get lonesome?"

"Damn straight, I do, but I'll bet you do, too. Tell the truth."

"Sometimes," she admitted, smiling at him. The moment her eyes met his, she felt the flash of awareness that surfaced every time they looked at each other. *He* might be numb from his divorce, but *she* wasn't. And he didn't act as if he was numb. When he talked about being lonely, she could hear the note of pain in his voice. As he looked at her, she saw a flicker in the depths of his eyes and wondered what thoughts were going through his mind. His gaze returned to the road.

"How far away do you think you parked?"

"Three hundred miles away."

His head snapped around and then he laughed. "Once again—serves you right for sneaking up on me. You're lucky you didn't run into wild animals."

"I was afraid I would. I even brought doggie treats in case you had a guard dog."

"You were on target there with my mutts, but if I'd had a real guard dog, you'd have been hamburger yourself before you could have tossed them doggie treats. Chicago, don't do that again!"

"I won't. I learned my lesson." She wondered about him, remembering everything Nessie had said and recalling the woman's statement, "Zach's got his problems." What were those problems? Loneliness? Temper? Hurt over Amber?

"There's a car off the road up ahead," he said, interrupting her thoughts.

"That's it," she said, looking at her black car parked at an angle beside a bushy spruce. "I can drive into town and then you won't have to—"

"Forget it. I'll take you to town." He slowed, pulled off the highway and halted near her car. They both climbed out of the pickup and moved through high grass together. A cool breeze tugged at Emily's hair, wound tightly on top of her head.

Zach turned to face her and held out his hand. "The ground is damp here. You might be bogged down. Give me your keys and I'll get your car up on the highway."

"I can drive my *own* car onto the highway."

"Chicago, you bristle anytime I try to do something for you," he said, amused that she didn't want him to take charge of anything involving her. Fire flashed in the depths of her green eyes as she gazed up at him. He couldn't resist looking at her mouth. The impulse to satisfy his curiosity was overwhelming. He was dancing on dynamite, yet he ignored reason. He reached out to tug lightly on wayward tendrils of hair that had escaped the bun and curled over her ear.

"I like your hair loose."

"I do my best to try to control it." Her breathless voice made his insides clutch.

"It's better down, like it was last night. Much better." He liked more than her tantalizing hair. A lot more. Yet the lady was off-limits. His life was complicated enough. A kiss would only heighten his awareness of lonely nights and an empty bed. He knew too well the hazards to his heart of getting entangled with a pretty woman.

But the arguments were feeble and useless. He wanted to know, to taste, to touch. From the moment he'd brought her into his house, he had wanted to kiss her and had been fighting the temptation. Now caution went with the wind.

While he watched her, he pushed his hat to the back of his head. Her face was raised to his, her mouth an irresistible invitation. He closed the distance between them, sliding his arm lightly around her waist. The moment he touched her, his insides tightened. He caught a lemony scent of soap in her hair.

Her faint protest was a syllable and then his lips silenced her. As his mouth met hers, he felt as if the earth had fallen out from under him. Her lips were soft, pliant beneath his. He brushed them so lightly, yet the touch shook him. Whatever volatile chemistry had sparked between them so many times when they merely looked at each other, now burst into scarlet flames with the touch of her mouth against his.

She stood stiffly, her hands against his upper arms, her lips closed. In her own quiet way she was fighting him, and damn well she should. But as he brushed his lips over hers a second time, he felt a change.

She closed her eyes and her body softened, fitting against him. The moment she moved closer, his heart lurched. He tightened his arms around her.

When his mouth covered hers firmly, hers opened to him. The tip of his tongue touched her lips and slid over her lower lip, touching her teeth, her tongue. Chemistry couldn't begin to explain the longing that swamped him.

Zach's kiss rocked Emily. She was out of her depth, drowning in a kiss that felt as if she had been waiting for it all her life. She was hot, her insides tightening, an ache throbbing deep within her, a need tearing at her. She heard herself moan faintly.

A tiny voice screamed that it wasn't fair for his kisses to be so great, so incredibly right. She should push him away. Instead, she slipped her arms around his waist, felt the hardness of his muscled chest pressed against her. She felt his arousal and knew his response was as intense as hers. Her fingers wound in his hair, the strands thick and smooth beneath her hands.

Zach held her as if she were made of crystal; he knew she had sore ribs and she seemed delicate. Yet her kisses and her response shook him. He had expected softness, sweetness. He had been wrong. Her kisses shattered him, making his breath stop and his heart pound and his blood roar. Time ceased and the world vanished, and all he was aware of was her. She was earthy and so responsive that he was stunned, feeling deep thrumming chords of need and desire. She kissed him back, her tongue curiously seeking.

A dim voice in his mind screamed that he should not be kissing her—this woman who had walked into his life out of a dark night and slipped past his defenses. He should keep his hands to himself. Yet he was already so deeply involved, he didn't want to get loose. And her kisses were so much more than he had expected or ever known—kisses that were hot breathy promises of passion.

And the kisses were escalating into a need that threatened to destroy too many things in their lives. He could feel her coming apart in his arms, and he was fully aroused, erotic images taunting him. She moaned softly, her body molding to his, her hips moving against him.

Zach knew he had to stop—she was his ex-sister-in-law.

But ignoring his own reasoning, he buried his hand in her hair, twisting his fingers in the soft locks, letting her kisses set him on fire.

Emily struggled for reason and caution. She hurt deep in her heart. She knew with a woman's intuition that she had found something special with Zach—something she would not find again with any other man. Yet a relationship with him was not hers to take or explore. From the hurt in his voice when he talked about Amber, Emily knew he was still in love with her sister. And all Amber had to do was to have a change of heart and walk back into his life. Which was the way it should be.

For only a moment longer, Emily kissed him back, wanting what she knew she could never have.

Wanting to hold him tightly, she slipped her hands to his shoulders instead and pushed against him. She opened her eyes to find him watching her, and trembled beneath the intensity in the depths of his brown eyes. No man had ever before looked at her in that manner. Her breasts tingled and her body ached with a need that couldn't be assuaged.

On a windy mountainside, in a place she had never been before and would never return to, she had found something she had sometimes dreamed about, but never really believed in. It was magical—yet it was the wrong place, the wrong time…the wrong person.

"We can't," she whispered, leaning away from him, feeling scalded by the heat in his eyes. A muscle worked in his jaw and he held her arms tightly while his gaze swept over her features.

"You're right. It won't happen again," he stated bluntly. His voice was breathless. His chest heaved as if he couldn't get any air. His dark eyes flashed with what looked like anger. He turned to head to his pickup. Emily watched him stride away—a tough, solitary cowboy, and yet so much more.

As he reached the door, he paused to look at her. Another pain tore at Zach's heart while he stared at the slender figure standing so still, her expression solemn, her big green eyes on him. Breezes tugged at her tangle of curls, and he wanted to stride back to her, to pull her into the woods and down on the damp needle-strewn ground, to take her. He wanted to bury himself in her softness, feel her body moving beneath his, feel those long, silky legs wrapped around him. He wanted her fire and her honesty.

"Damn it," he muttered beneath his breath. She looked so alone. She looked fragile. He had to tell himself that she wasn't. She was a strong woman, filled with purpose, in charge of her life. Then why did he want to go wrap his arms around her and hold her against his heart?

"You go ahead. I'll follow you home," he said, and without waiting for her answer, yanked open the door and climbed into his pickup.

He watched her slide behind the wheel of her own car. She eased out competently without miring in the damp earth and in minutes drove past him without looking his way. He swung around in a U-turn and followed her.

"Why didn't I meet you first?" he said aloud, but then thought of his children and knew he wouldn't have things any other way. He adored Rebecca and Jason. But never once had kisses with Amber been what he had just experienced with Emily.

"Damn it!" His fist hit the steering wheel. "I swear," he said aloud, "I will never again compare them."

Amber was out of his life and he wanted her to stay that way. Emily would go out of it soon enough and he knew he had to let her go. As if he would have a choice—it was obvious she wanted no part of him. And their heart-stopping, slow-burning, soul-matching kisses wouldn't change their futures.

He had work to do at home and he never wanted to see Amber again. Yet, against his better judgment, he was going to help Emily search for her.

He followed Emily until she stopped in front of his garage. Long legs swung out of the car and she stood, coming toward him with a saucy twist of her hips and a bounce of her breasts that held his attention riveted and reminded him of their kisses. Did she have the remotest idea of the power of those kisses?

Her hair was loose now, blowing in the morning breeze and destroying that neat, prim look she tried to achieve. She carried her suitcase and motioned toward the house, disappearing inside while he sat smoldering, remembering their passionate encounter.

Emily reappeared a few minutes later and crossed the yard to the car. Once again she was bandbox neat in a white silk blouse, a navy skirt and pumps. Her hair was again secured in a bun on her head, and she seemed wound up just as tight. Yet earlier when their lips had met, she had more than let her defenses down. She had responded to his kisses as if she had been waiting for them forever.

The woman said she seldom dated. Bah, humbug to that one! He opened the door for her and she climbed up beside him. "I'm ready."

"Yeah, so am I," he answered gruffly, resisting the urge to pull the pins from her hair and let the silky mass free. She turned to give him a wide-eyed stare as if she realized he had something else on his mind. Beneath his gaze, her cheeks turned pink.

Zach turned the pickup and headed toward the highway again. They wound up through the mountains on a beautiful morning that Emily barely noticed. Her attention was focused on the man only a few feet from her—the man whose passion had shaken her badly.

Of all the people on earth to have such a shattering effect on her, why *him?* How long would it take her mouth to stop tingling, her mind to forget the moment his arms held her tightly? She didn't want Zach's kisses, didn't want them to be unforgettable, life-changing. Yet they had been. How long would it take to forget them once she was back in Chicago? As long as she lived, she suspected. She would remember and long for something she could never have.

Now I'm numb. He hadn't acted numb. Far from it. He had breathed slowly like a man savoring life, and he'd looked at her with enough heat to start a fire. Her pulse was drumming simply from the memory. She glanced at him to find him looking at her. Then his attention went back to the road, and she noticed that his knuckles on the steering wheel were white.

What was running through his mind? Was he angry over going to town to search for Amber? While he hadn't acted *numb,* she knew he couldn't possibly be as shaken and disturbed by their kisses as she was. She had little to compare it with. He had plenty.

Her mind snapped shut. She didn't want to think about Zach's past. If she had any sense, she would blot Zach Durham and his kisses out of her mind. She would pray she could find Amber and go home. Maybe by the time they got to town, Sheriff Nunez would have located Amber, happily enjoying herself, and Emily could go home and start trying to forget the man she could never have.

Zach drove down to a level stretch of land and within minutes had slowed to enter the small town of San Luis. Bathed in warm morning sunshine, cottonwoods and willows lined the dusty streets. Bright red and pink hollyhocks bloomed in front of adobe houses. He slowed even more as they reached the stretch of two blocks that held the town's business buildings. He parked in front of the sheriff's office and climbed out of the pickup to come around and meet her. As they stood on the sidewalk in the sleepy town, Emily tried to curb her response to this man—his hat pushed to the back of his head, brown locks of hair falling on his forehead.

"Let's get this over with." Zach took her arm and led her into the building. The desk sergeant greeted them and called the sheriff on the intercom.

A short time later Emily saw the heavy-set sheriff come out of an office.

"Morning, Miss Stockton," he said politely, curiosity

filling his blue eyes as he glanced back and forth between them. "Morning, Zach," he said, shaking hands with the cowboy. "Come into my office."

They followed him into a small room with file cabinets, a map of the county on one wall, vinyl chairs and a metal desk littered with papers.

"Have a seat," the sheriff said as he moved behind his desk and plopped down, leaning back in a chair that squeaked. "I can tell you right now, Miss Stockton, we don't know where your sister is. Last night we ran her picture on the news and my men are out now asking questions. The minute we turn up anything, I'll let you know."

"Thank you. I asked a few questions myself and I have a list of names the bartender at the Red Rocket gave me."

Zach pulled the list from his pocket. "I talked Emily out of trying to question these men herself."

Bill Nunez leaned forward to take the list, glanced at it and looked at Zach with raised eyebrows. "Glad you did." His gaze shifted to Emily. "Just leave the search to the officials, Miss Stockton. We're trained to do this, and we're efficient—even though it may not look like it to you."

He dropped the list on a pile of papers before his gaze rested on Zach.

"I had some questions, but seeing you two on a friendly basis eliminates a lot of them. I assume you have discussed all you know about Amber."

"Yes," Zach said. "But I'll answer any questions you still have."

"Good. I'd like to go over some things with you since you were the last one seen talking to Amber. Tell me again about that night at the bar."

Emily turned in the seat to listen to Zach talk. His voice was flat and impasssive, yet she knew seeing Amber again had stirred up his emotions.

After thirty minutes Nunez turned to Emily. "Miss Stockton, if you have any other questions, I'll be happy to answer them. If not, you don't have to sit here while we go over all this.''

"I just wanted to see if you had any leads.''

"I told you, I'll call when I do.''

She stood and both men came to their feet. ''I'll leave, then.'' She looked at Zach. ''I know you have to go by the grocery. I'll meet you there.''

"Sure. How long do you think we'll be?'' he asked Nunez.

"Another twenty or thirty minutes ought to be enough time.''

"See you in thirty minutes at the grocery,'' Zach said.

"Thanks, Sheriff,'' Emily said and left, closing the door behind her. She immediately headed for the beauty salon she had seen in the next block. Maybe someone there could help her to locate Amber.

A half hour later, Emily stood at the grocery, waiting for Zach. When she saw him coming across the street, her pulse jumped just at the sight of him.

"Nunez has men working on the case.''

"But not getting anywhere. I'd like to talk to a few more people here in town. Amber is the kind of woman people notice.''

"Yeah, I know. I'll ask around, too.'' He glanced at his watch. ''You check out of the hotel and put your things in the pickup. I'll meet you back here in an hour. I have a grocery list. If you get here first, pick up the groceries for me and tell them I'll be in to pay for them, then I won't have to take the time to get them later. Here are the keys to the pickup.''

"Sure.''

He caught her chin, his warm fingers causing tingles to dance inside her. ''You're laughing at me.''

"I'm just so unaccustomed to being told what to do. I can't recall a time.''

"Surely when you were little, your mom or dad bossed you around.''

She shook her head. "I've been telling Mom what to do for as long as I can remember. My dad wasn't around much, thank heaven. I can remember standing on a chair to cook and wash dishes."

"Amber has to be the oldest," he said, running his finger along her jaw.

"She is. She's thirty this year and I'm twenty-eight."

"You have an impressive job for someone twenty-eight," he said, his fingers moving down to her shoulder.

"Thank you. I've worked hard."

"Where's your mother now?"

"In drug rehab. She's been there before and it may not do any more good this time than other times, but I have to try. I always have to try with my family. You should understand that. You're helping Nessie tremendously. You care for your kids."

"I started to say, 'What parent wouldn't?' but we both know the answer to that one."

"I don't understand Amber...but then I've never understood any of my family."

His fingers trailed over her ear. "Maybe you don't have the same father."

"I suggested that once to my mom and she exploded. She slapped me and said I did have the same father." Emily was growing too aware of Zach standing so close to her, his fingers lightly stroking her ear while he watched her intently.

"That's a strong reaction unless she hit you often."

"No, she didn't. For her, it was a violent reaction."

"That might not be the truth, then."

Emily shrugged. "I'll never know."

"Do you look like them?"

"Not even remotely. Amber looks like Mom. Mom is a beautiful woman—or she was." Not wanting to continue the conversation in the direction it was headed, Emily motioned to her own watch and abruptly said, "Let's get started. I'll see you in an hour."

Emily entered the cool interior of the hotel and crossed to the desk to pay her bill and check out. While she waited, she glanced out the window and watched Zach cross the street. The tall cowboy with the black hat was easy to spot since he towered above most people.

When she was done, she left to talk to some more people in town—starting this time at the bank—to ask if anyone had seen Amber. But she didn't turn up any further clues.

An hour later Emily stood in the checkout line at the grocery. She felt a prickle across her back and turned to find Zach headed toward her, his gaze meeting hers. Her heart jumped and she tried to ignore the sprint in her pulse as he strode up to her.

"We timed this just right. I'll pay for these and get them into the pickup." He turned to the blond checker. "Hi, Beth."

"Hi, Mr. Durham. Haven't seen you in a while."

"Haven't needed groceries in a while," he answered pleasantly.

"I added a few things of my own. They're in the next basket," Emily said.

"I'll get them. Beth, just put those with mine."

"I don't suppose it will do any good to argue with you," Emily said, aware the checker was watching them intently.

"Not a bit."

She waited quietly until they were alone in the truck. "I think the checker is curious about who I am and why I was with you."

"You shouldn't care. And rumors will be squelched fast as Nunez talks to people. Everyone will know you're Amber's sister in town looking for her." Zach backed the truck away from the curb and swung around to head home, stopping at the light.

"Did you learn anything?"

"Sorry, nothing's turned up so far."

She felt her hopes plummet. "I asked every place I could think she might have gone. If Amber was around, a hair salon would be the first place she'd go, but no one has seen her. I hoped you'd learn something. I thought maybe by now the police would have found some trace of her.''

"Sorry, nothing yet, but they're still working. Stoney's here in town, but he was arrested for slashing Jake Wilken's tires and stealing his CD player from his car. He was in jail all that week after Amber was seen at the bar, and he was in jail when her car was burned.''

"So that rules him out absolutely.'' Emily glanced outside, seeing the bullet-ridden sign that proclaimed San Luis's city limits, population 758, elevation 5,400 feet.

''The sheriff asked me where I was the night her car burned.''

Emily twisted in the seat to watch him. She had wondered the same thing, but hadn't asked. He had pushed his hat to the back of his head again.

''I was home with my kids. But they would make lousy witnesses.''

''I believe you,'' she answered solemnly, knowing that she did.

''I'm making progress winning your trust,'' he remarked quietly. He reached across the seat to touch her chin. It was a light, almost impersonal touch, yet after their hot kisses, no contact could be impersonal. ''Don't worry until you have to. You know Amber is probably doing what she wants right now.''

''Sometimes I think that, but then I remember being told about her car. Sheriff Nunez said someone doused it in gasoline and set it on fire. Where was Amber when that happened?''

''I don't know, Emily, but we will find out.'' He frowned and returned his attention to the street. ''Meanwhile, you have to keep up your strength. How about getting some lunch?'' he asked, parking in front of the café.

''I'm ready to eat,'' she answered.

They went inside a long, narrow café and sat in a booth to order *quesadillas* and ice water. Zach talked about the kids and his plans to send them to the county school when they were older.

"Enough about the Durhams. Where in Chicago do you live, Emily?"

"I work in downtown Chicago so I have a condo rather close by. It's a small one-bedroom place, no pets. I'd like a dog, but I don't have the time for one. It's nice you have dogs for the children."

"All our dogs and cats were strays that I found abandoned. We're getting a menagerie, but the cats live around the barn. And the kids love the dogs and the dogs love the kids."

"That's good, Zach."

He studied her, igniting something inside her. She wondered what he was thinking. "A penny for your thoughts."

"I can't get over how different you are from your sister," he answered quietly.

"For most of her life, Emily might have taken the comparison badly, but this time she knew it was a compliment. "Thank you."

They ate and sat talking until she noticed they were the only customers in the place. "Zach, maybe they would like to close."

He glanced around. "They stay open all day, but I better head back to the ranch. We're moving calves to another pasture and I should check on things."

They left, climbed into his pickup and headed out of town, racing along a winding road that stretched up into the mountains. Gray-tinted clouds were boiling over the tall peaks, and she suspected they would get afternoon showers.

Ten miles later they drove through a brief rain shower, but as they curved up between mountains, they drove back into sunshine.

When they arrived at the ranch house, a pickup was parked at the back gate. Beneath two tall aspens in the yard, the children played with a ball and the dogs ran after them, afternoon sunshine spilling over the scene. Emily felt a pang. It looked like a dream, a home and family she had never known or had. She could never recall running and playing with Amber, having a pet, or even having a home for more than a few months at a stretch.

"You have a beautiful place here," she said.

Zach cut the motor and turned to look at her. He heard the wistful note in her voice and gazed at her profile as she watched the children.

"Your sister thought it was a prison," he said, realizing that for the first time he didn't feel scalding bitterness when he thought about Amber. Lately she'd receded from his conscious thoughts to a past that maybe someday he could look back on without such pain.

"I've never lived in a house. It was always apartments, and still is."

"I love it here even if it is damned lonely now."

He climbed out and went around as Emily stepped out and closed the pickup door. Her gaze was still on the children. He wondered about her past: if she had to care for Amber, and a mother who must have been like Amber, and a father who was even worse, there must not have been many carefree moments in her life. Maybe that explained the solemnity that seemed to cloak her.

They crossed the drive to the gate while the dogs barked a frenzied greeting and the children ran to meet them. As soon as Zach opened the gate, the dogs and the children threw themselves at him.

"Get down!" Zach ordered the dogs, picking up Jason, then Rebecca, then giving them each a squeeze. As soon as he set them on their feet, they raced to a sandbox.

Nessie stood by the fence, her straight black hair blowing slightly. Beside her was a brown-skinned cowboy in a dusty T-shirt and jeans, whose black hair and prominent cheekbones proclaimed his Native American heritage. He gazed at Emily with a polite smile.

"Emily, this is Quint Colton," Zach said. "Quint, meet Emily Stockton."

"Howdy," Quint replied with a flash of a smile. He was several inches shorter than Zach, yet still over six feet tall. A scar slashed across his cheek and another on his jaw. She noticed the hand resting on the fence was missing two fingers.

"Glad to meet you," she responded politely.

"Emily is Amber's sister," Zach explained.

"My sister has disappeared and I'm here searching for her," she added quickly.

"If you hear anything, let us know," Zach added.

"Sure. Haven't heard anything yet, though. Sorry, ma'am." Quint's dark-eyed gaze shifted to Zach. "We've got the calves moved to the north pasture. I just finished and stopped by here."

"Good."

"Supper's about cooked," Nessie said. "All you have to do is take it out of the oven and put it on the table."

"Stay and eat with us," Zach told her. "You, too, if you want, Quint."

"Thanks. I'll eat down at the house," Quint said.

"Please stay," Emily added to Nessie.

"If you don't mind," she replied, glancing at Quint, "I'll take some to my place to eat."

"Sure. Whatever you want. We'll wash up," Zach said, taking Emily's arm and turning for the house.

"It was nice to have met you," Emily said to Quint.

"Thank you, ma'am," he replied, nodding. "Nice to meet you."

As Emily turned toward the house, she was aware of Zach lightly holding her arm. She walked close beside him, her long legs matching his stride.

"Quint looks rather tough."

"He's tough as granite. He lost two fingers in a knife fight several years ago."

Emily shivered and wondered about Zach and the men who worked for him. "Do you ride in rodeos?"

"Yep."

"Why? Why would you want to go through all that? No one forces you to."

He grinned. "It's a challenge. To see if I can."

"And maybe Nessie's not quite as numb as you thought."

"Because Quint's here? He stops to talk to her a lot lately, so maybe you're right. I'll bet she won't rush into any relationship, though. And Quint's pretty much his own man. He keeps part of himself shut away from others."

"We all do that," she answered lightly, and he turned to look down at her.

"Oh, Zach," Nessie called, waving her hand. "I almost forgot. I remembered something today. It didn't seem important at the time and I forgot about it until after you left this morning. I was thinking about Emily being here to find her sister."

"What is it?" Zach asked, dropping Emily's arm and turning.

"About a week after you saw Amber in the bar, a man called here one morning asking for her."

Five

"**O**ne morning while you were gone, the phone rang," Nessie continued. "I answered and a man's voice said, 'Amber.' I told him that I wasn't Amber. The phone clicked and that was it."

"That was the only call?"

"Yes. That's why it didn't seem important at the time. Sorry if I should have told you—"

"Forget it," Zach said. "You remembered it, and I'll tell Nunez. Thanks, Nessie."

She smiled and turned to talk with Quint.

"When she called me, Amber said someone was after her. Maybe he found her," Emily said, a knot forming in her stomach.

"Try not to worry too much until you know something for sure," he said. Zach wanted to place his arm across her shoulders. Instead, he clenched his fists and jammed them into his pockets to keep from reaching for her. Why did he continually have this urge to touch her? He knew it wasn't frustration, or his current celibate state. Otherwise, he would have had the same reaction to Nessie.

Emily had been right about Nessie—the woman was attractive—yet he felt toward her as he would toward a sister. Not this prickly awareness he suffered with Emily that kept his temperature at jungle heat. And he had barely thought about the ranch today—something that hadn't ever happened before. He never took off work unless he had to get the kids into town for doctors' appointments or to get clothes.

Something nagged at him and he shifted his thoughts, trying and failing, too preoccupied with Emily to think of much else.

They entered the house, which smelled inviting, and he crossed the room to glance in the oven at Nessie's casserole. Golden ears of corn were on the kitchen counter, and a pan was ready in which to cook them.

He crossed the room to the fridge and noticed the tossed salad as he withdrew a beer to offer to Emily.

"Beer?"

"No, thanks. If you have iced tea, I'll take that."

"Sure." He fixed a glass of tea, handed it to her and leaned against the counter. "I've been thinking about what Nessie told us about that call. After I saw Amber in the bar that Saturday night, for the next few nights, the phone would ring. When I'd answer, the other person would hang up without saying a word. I didn't give it any thought before. Figured it was wrong numbers—or kids. But it could have been someone who thought Amber went home with me and who was calling, hoping she would answer. When she didn't, the caller would hang up."

"And when Nessie answered, the caller not only learned Amber wasn't here, but also probably thought you had another woman living with you," Emily finished.

"That's a possibility. I haven't gotten any more of those calls, and now I think we know why. So the person looking for Amber might have moved on, thinking Amber was no longer around here. Or he might still be searching." Zach set down the beer. "I'll call Nunez and tell him. He can mull it over."

"I need to phone home and check with my office."

"You can use the phone in my office. Come on. Now that I think about it, you've never seen the whole house."

As Emily moved from room to room, glancing in the dining room with its large mahogany table and a fireplace at one end, looking at the living room she had been in so briefly the night before, the bathroom, and finally his office, she was aware of the masculine decor.

"It doesn't look as if Amber ever lived here," she remarked as she stood inside his office and gazed at the massive rosewood desk, Navaho rug, and western art on the walls. "Did you remove her things or do the house over?"

"Neither, except in our bedroom. When she left, she took her things, but she had been like a gypsy passing through my life. She had little interest in making friends with neighbors. She didn't care to entertain. She didn't care about the house. From the first, she was bored out here. She had a huge collection of videos that I took down to the bunkhouse when she left. Jewelry was her thing. And clothes."

"I'm not surprised. Jewelry and clothes have always been all she was interested in. But I thought maybe when she married, she changed."

"I inherited this place from my grandfather. The dining room is like it was when he lived here. He left a lot of furniture, including his desk, the rug and the leather chair in here."

"Do you have brothers or sisters?" she asked, realizing how little she knew about him.

"I have a brother who is finishing college and will help Dad run the Texas ranch. Dad's health isn't great and Sean will step in as soon as he graduates at the end of the summer. I have a sister, Alissa, who is married and is a nurse in Houston, and has two boys in elementary school."

"Nice family."

"They barely knew Amber. We went home a few times, but then Amber stopped going with me. So what about your family? I don't know much beyond the little that you told me."

"Dad's in prison for robbery and fraud. He was abusive to my mother and we were glad when he was sent away. Mom holds odd jobs—waitress, clerk, whatever she can...when she's clean and sober. But right now she's in drug rehab in Chicago. Her health isn't too good. There's just Amber and me. I have a grandmother who is normal, but my grandfather was in trouble with the law, too. We are a classic dysfunctional family."

"I'm surprised you didn't just walk away from it all."

"It's the only family I have. Besides, someone always needed attention."

"My family is close. Amber could never understand that. I take the kids back to Texas on holidays. I want them to know their aunt and uncle, grandparents and great-grandparents. Mom's parents still live in Texas. Family is important to me."

"Then be thankful you have a family like yours and not like mine. I can't remember a holiday we all spent together. Nor do I want to."

Both of them had lonely lives, Zach realised. His nights were empty and his days were often spent alone. "How do you spend your holidays?"

"I have friends. If they're busy, I help at the shelter. They always need someone extra on holidays. And don't look at me like you think I'm missing out on life. I'm very busy and satisfied. I love my job and living in Chicago."

"I imagine you do," he said quietly, his eyes intent on her, making her pulse jump. She remembered the morning, and how swiftly she had been in his arms. He looked as if he was on the verge of wrapping his arms around her again right now. And she wanted him to.

He ran his fingers along the desk and stepped back from

her. His breathing had become irregular and he was re-
garding her with a tenderness that he had shown before
only for his children.

"Make your calls. We'll have supper in about thirty
minutes, all right?"

"Yes."

He crossed the room and closed the door.

She looked at his desk, strewn with papers, and suspected
he preferred working outside to sitting in his office doing
bookkeeping. It was a disturbing mess that she wanted to
straighten, but she resisted, guessing he enjoyed clutter as
much as she enjoyed order.

For a moment, she couldn't find the phone, but then she
unearthed it beneath a stack of papers. She noticed a pile
of medical bills and remembered Nessie's remark about
Zach having problems. Despite her curiosity, she moved
the phone and picked up the receiver to call her office.

Supper was lively, with Jason and Rebecca both wanting
to chatter about the afternoon. Again Emily noticed how
relaxed Zach was with the children, helping them with their
meals. She glanced at him often and caught him studying
her. She wondered whether he gave any thought to their
kisses or not.

As soon as the children finished dinner, Zach washed
their hands. "Can we play outside?" Rebecca asked.

"Will you swing us?" Jason clapped his hands.

"Go out with them," Emily said, standing to clear the
table. "I'll clean these plates and come out."

"Let's reverse that order if you can stand the little tykes.
And I'll do this cleaning," he said, taking a plate. "Give
you a choice—outside with the urchins, or sit and watch
me clean while they wait for both of us."

"I'll take them outside if that's what you want," she
said, drawing cheers from Rebecca, who took Emily's hand
in her small one.

Emily stepped outside into the cool night air. She had

changed to her jeans, a T-shirt and sneakers, and she felt relaxed and happy with Zach and the children. The sun was still in the sky and it was a refreshing time of day. Jason toddled to the swing and waited expectantly. She lifted him up and buckled him in. "You go first and then Rebecca gets to swing."

"Up high, over your head," he begged, kicking his short legs, the laces from his sneakers flapping in the wind.

She pushed, glancing around to see Rebecca in the sandbox, busily patting a mound of sand. Emily swung Jason, who seemed content. When she asked Rebecca if she wanted a turn, Rebecca shook her head, but asked for a bedtime story later. After a few more minutes, Jason wanted down and rushed to join Rebecca in the sandbox. Emily sat on one of the lawn chairs, enjoying a silence that was deep, broken only by the chirping of birds. Emily experienced a sense of peace, and wondered again how Amber could so easily have thrown this life away.

The slap of the screen door made her look up, and she watched as Zach crossed the lawn. Her pulse jumped at the sight of him. The wind tangled his brown hair. He had rolled his sleeves high on his arms and unbuttoned the front of his shirt to his waist. He dropped down on the grass and stretched out with one knee bent. "Have they driven you crazy?"

"Not at all. I promised Rebecca I would read a story to them when we go inside."

"I'll bet, Chicago—city girl that you are—you've never stretched out in the grass on a summer evening."

She accepted the challenge, kicked off her shoes and slid down beside him to sit with her legs folded under her.

"That isn't stretched out," he observed with a grin.

"Don't you get ants in your hair?"

"Never have so far," he answered with amusement. "Lie down and look at the clouds with me."

She eased onto the grass, aware of his lanky body stretched only inches away, his shirt open and revealing his broad chest. White clouds, stark against the clear blue sky, moved lazily overhead, shapes changing as she watched.

"There, see, it looks like a dog."

"I don't see any such thing," she answered, listening to the rumble of his bass voice.

With squeals and shouts the children descended on them. Rebecca plopped on Emily while Jason threw himself on Zach. He laughed and sat up, scooping Rebecca off Emily.

"Hey! You little varmints! Rebecca, you've got sand all over your aunt!"

"I'm all right," Emily said, laughing and sitting up to brush sand off her middle.

"You rascals," he teased, holding both of the screeching, wriggling children. "I know what I'll do with you." Holding one under each arm, he ran across the yard to a red aluminum wheelbarrow beside a metal shed. He set the children in the wheelbarrow in what Emily realized must be a familiar game. They both clutched the sides and laughed while Zach grabbed up the handles and ran across the yard, pushing them. They screamed in delight when he turned in a loop, laughing each time they hit bumps.

Watching them, Emily smiled at the long-legged cowboy who looked like a kid himself. It was almost impossible to think he was the same man who had questioned her so fiercely last night or kissed her so passionately this morning. And he was a wonderful father to his children.

They raced full tilt toward Emily, who threw up her hands and ran. She glanced over her shoulder to see them gaining on her and sprinted ahead, dodging behind a tree as they barreled past. When they finally halted, Zach gently dumped the children onto the ground.

"We'll walk down and look at the horses and then it's—" he lowered his voice, "bath time."

Howls of protest went up about the baths, but they grabbed his hands and tugged him toward the gate. His gaze went past them to Emily. "Want to walk down to the barn?"

"Love to," she said, joining them. She felt a small tug as Rebecca slipped a hand into hers. Emily's heart missed a beat and she held the tiny hand, feeling a rush of warmth for the children. Longing for a family like this assailed her, and she shifted her thoughts, knowing it was a dangerous path to follow.

They spent some time looking at horses, and Zach let the children ride a gentle mare, which he led around the corral. Bath time arrived but Rebecca's protests died when Emily volunteered to oversee the ritual.

When they were in pajamas, smelling of soap and warm from bathing, Emily held both of them in her lap and read three stories to them, aware of Zach's gaze on her. He listened as raptly as did the children. Yet she wondered what was really going through his mind.

When story time was over, they each picked up a child to carry to bed, and Emily again felt a strange pull on her heart as Rebecca's arms closed around her neck. How easily both children had accepted her. Particularly Rebecca.

"Aunt Emily, I like you here," Rebecca said softly, as Emily sat on the side of the bed. "Will you stay?"

"I can't stay always, but I'll be here another day at least. I'll come back to see you."

"You will?"

"Yes, I will."

"Mommy left and she didn't come back."

"I'm sorry." She paused, then added, "I promise I will come back."

Rebecca smiled and looked past Emily, who glanced around to see Zach standing only yards behind her. For a man whose boot heels clattered constantly on bare wood floors, he could move with complete stealth when he chose to. She brushed a kiss across Rebecca's forehead and moved away. "Good night, Rebecca."

"'Night, Aunt Emily," said a small voice and then Emily heard the rumble of Zach's voice as he sat down to talk to Rebecca.

Emily went to Jason's room and spent a few minutes telling him good-night before going downstairs to the family room.

As Zach was entering the room a short time later, the phone rang. He picked it up and Emily couldn't help hearing his part of the conversation. She met his gaze as she listened to "yes" and "no" answers, and then a thank-you. He replaced the receiver.

"With so many questions being asked in town word is spreading. That was a guy who works on one of the ranches around here. He said he thinks someone has seen Amber in the past week in the Full Moon bar that's on the highway near Colbert."

"That would be *since* her car burned! Thank God!"

Zach nodded, rubbing the back of his neck. "Even though he said he called Nunez with the information, I think I'll drive out to that bar tonight and ask a few questions. You can stay home, or if you want to go, I'll call Nessie to come stay with the kids."

"I'd like to go," she said, anxious to find out about Amber. Could her sister still be in the area? "Will Nessie tell you if she doesn't want to stay, or can't stay?"

"Sure." He called a number and almost immediately it was arranged that Nessie would be right over.

"I want to change," Emily said, heading toward the door.

"Wear your jeans. I'll warn you now, this is a rough place."

She nodded and left the room. She showered, then dressed in her jeans and a cotton blouse. Working as swiftly as she could, she redid her hair, brushing it and pinning it in a bun on top of her head.

It's better down like it was last night. She remembered Zach's husky voice as he had pushed his fingers into her hair, but she continued securing it on top of her head. This style felt best.

She yanked up her purse and hurried to the kitchen where

she heard voices. Zach stood talking to Nessie, who held a textbook beneath her arm. His gaze flicked over Emily and her pulse skittered.

"Hi, Nessie," Emily said, watching Zach turn away.

'Hi. You're going to look for your sister?" With her hands on her hips, Nessie was studying her like a slab of meat in the grocery.

"Yes." Emily sensed something was wrong and wondered what. She glanced at Zach, who was gathering up keys and jamming his billfold into his pocket.

"Emily, would you like a suggestion?" Nessie asked politely as she set the book on a chair.

"Yes," Emily answered, mystified.

"Zach, give us a minute," Nessie said, and motioned to Emily to follow her. "Let's go down to my house and let me get you something different to wear. You look like a Sunday school teacher, and you'll stand out in this dump like a baby rabbit in a snake pit." She looked up at Emily. "Do you mind?"

"No. That's fine. I want someone to tell us about Amber so whatever it takes...."

Nessie stopped abruptly, her hand on the screen door. "Before we go, run up to your room and get those pumps you wore today, and your stockings."

Emily retrieved them and left with Nessie. They hurried across the drive and past the barn to a small house with a light burning inside. Nessie unlocked the door and motioned to Emily to enter. She stepped inside a house filled with pictures and posters and colorful pillows on the chairs and sofa. Books were strewn over the room and a braided oval rug covered the plank floor.

"Come into my room and let's find something else for you to wear."

"Zach said jeans—"

"The jeans are fine. It's your starched white shirt that makes you look like a Girl Scout," Nessie said, leading the way to a bedroom with a rumpled, unmade bed and clothes strewn about. "Put on your stockings and wear those shoes with heels instead of your sneakers."

Rummaging in a drawer, she turned with a satisfied, "Here," and tossed a red T-shirt to Emily. Emily caught it and looked at the shirt. "This is way too small. You and I aren't the same size."

"Let's see. Put it on. You want to go without a bra?"

"No!"

"All right." Nessie grinned and turned to search in another drawer.

Emily changed shirts, then turned to look at herself in the mirror. The red T-shirt clung like a second skin and exposed inches of bare midriff. She had to laugh. "I told you—"

"It's great for where you're going."

"You're kidding," Emily said in astonishment, looking at her reflection. "In heels and jeans, I look all legs. I'm six feet tall. I look ridiculous."

"No, you don't. I know these guys. Just let me get you ready." Nessie tugged on her hand. "Sit down and let me put some makeup on you and comb your hair."

Biting back a protest, Emily shut her mouth and sat. She thought of Amber's style, and wondered what Zach would think. "Nessie, this is what I've worked all my life to get away from."

"What's that?" Nessie asked as she applied eye liner and eye shadow.

"Looking wild and like I want a man. I grew up in a neighborhood where too many girls tried to look this way too young—my sister included. I've tried to avoid it every way possible."

"I'd say you succeeded," Nessie said dryly, then applied blush and mascara.

"This isn't me," Emily insisted.

"It's only for a few hours," the younger woman retorted. They lapsed into silence while Nessie brushed, combed and fluffed out Emily's hair. "With this hair, I couldn't bear to braid it and pin it up in a bun."

"It's unmanageable."

"It's great. What curls! Wow! Think what Rebecca has to look forward to. I'd love all these curls."

"Not if you tried to do something with them. I can't go to work like this."

"Maybe not, but you can go dancing this way. And I'm betting those guys will answer every question you ask. Quint said he stays away from the bar you're going to."

"Quint looks tough enough for any bar," Emily remarked, watching Nessie in the mirror.

"He is. He's another one Zach's helped. Probably everyone on this ranch is. Okay, I'm done. *Voila!*"

Emily turned to stare at her reflection, feeling a shock. "I can't go out like this," she said, unaware of even having spoken aloud. Her hair was a mass of ringlets spilling over her shoulders, falling around her face. It was combed out from her head so it looked as if she had twice as much hair as usual. The shirt was too tight, too short; it outlined her breasts without leaving anything to the imagination. She was wearing huge gold hoop earrings that dangled over her shoulders and showed in spite of the mane of hair. And she had never worn so much makeup in her life. "I look like—"

"Yeah, you do. Every man in the place will want to talk to you. This way you might find out something about your sister."

Emily looked at Nessie. "This isn't me, but thank you. I don't know if I can carry this off."

"Just be a woman." Nessie grinned. "I hope, for your sake, Amber's all right."

"Thanks. We're not very close, really, but I have to try to find her."

"She hurt him and the children terribly," Nessie said solemnly. "He isn't over her yet."

"My sister has always done exactly what she wanted to. But she's still my sister."

"You're not like her. She wouldn't even hug her own children. She didn't want them messing her up."

"I didn't know you were here when she was."

"I wasn't. I've heard the men talk and the children tell me things and Zach has told me things. I know they're telling the truth."

"I'm sure they are."

"You're nothing like the woman I heard them tell about."

"You don't know me that well," Emily said, but she was glad Nessie saw her as different from Amber.

"You let the children hug you. That's enough for me."

"Thanks," Emily replied, feeling a warmth toward the woman and sensing she had a friend. "I want to come back to see them. Amber never wrote, and I didn't think I was wanted here."

"That's good to hear. They're sweeties and Zach's trying to make up for her absence. He's doing a good job, but he doesn't know it. He worries about them constantly, and he's lonely. It'll do him good to get out tonight. One more thing and then we're ready," Nessie said, spraying cologne generously. Emily fanned the air.

"Enough!"

Nessie laughed. "Let's go. We'll see what kind of reaction we get from the house male."

"The cologne may knock him senseless."

"It won't be the cologne."

They hurried back to the house and entered the kitchen, where Zach was wrapping an electrical cord with tape. He had changed to a black T-shirt. He glanced around at them, then his attention went to Emily. His hand holding the tape halted in midair, while the electrical cord fell unnoticed out of his other hand to the floor. He inhaled, his chest expanding as his gaze drifted over her in an assessment that made her cheeks flame.

"Jeez," he said quietly.

"See, I told you," Nessie whispered with satisfaction then headed toward the living room. "Y'all be careful. As soon as you go, I'll lock up and set the alarm."

Emily was barely aware of what Nessie had said. She was riveted beneath Zach's appraisal. His dark eyes flashed with fire and he dropped the tape on the counter without taking his eyes from her. She felt as if she were stripped bare beneath his searing look. Her pulse raced and her breasts tingled. Her nipples tightened and she knew it was as obvious as if the shirt hadn't existed.

Zach crossed the room to her, his eyes drifting over her like fingers touching her, lingering, and then coming back to look into her eyes. With every step he took, her pulse raced faster until her pounding heart was deafening. He stopped only inches from her.

"I better take a club. I'll have to fight every guy in the bar."

She had no idea whether she answered him or not. He looked admiringly at her hair and touched a curl, pulling it lightly.

Zach couldn't stop staring at her. The transformation was startling, and he could feel his body reacting swiftly to her. Beneath the prim strait-laced social worker was a woman who could melt a man—and then burn him to ashes.

This morning he had wanted to kiss her. Now he wanted to take her to bed. The T-shirt revealed her figure, showing the reaction she was having to him—and it took his breath away. He knew he should be doing something besides standing here staring at her while he fought bodily urges and more. Much more. The woman was all the things he thought a woman should be—warmhearted, intelligent, loving with the children. Only, damn it, she was the wrong woman to be all those things. She was still as off-limits to him as if she had a husband standing beside her with his arm around her.

Only it wasn't a husband who was the barrier. It was her

bloodline. He would never again get involved with Amber or any part of her. Especially an ex-sister-in-law who was loyal to her sister. Never.

But why was he rooted to the spot, unable to find his voice, unable to stop staring or touching Emily?

"You clean up good, Chicago," he said in a husky voice.

"I'm not sure I'm supposed to say thank-you. This isn't exactly cleaned up."

"All right, you mess up good. I'm about to go up in flames."

"Then let's get you out into the cool night air."

"At the moment I don't want to go any farther than about twelve inches from where I'm standing."

"You have to."

"Yeah."

They stood without moving. Emily's heart thudded beneath his intense stare, and she couldn't turn away. "Zach?"

"After you," he said in a husky voice that touched her like a caress. With an effort, she looked away and headed for the door, her heart pounding and her back tingling. She knew she was still under his scalding scrutiny.

Zach watched her walk to the door. The jeans were tight, her walk a sexy sway. He mentally stripped away the clothing. He inhaled, unable to hear anything for the roaring in his ears. There was nothing coy, calculating or fake about her. Emily looked like a woman of passion—earthy, fiery— and when her big green eyes focused on him, all the straightforward honesty in her was clearly revealed. It was a lethal combination and he wondered whether he would get through the night.

He knew he would never look at her the same way again.

He reminded himself that he had to try to look at her just one way—as his ex-sister-in-law. He had been blindsided by a woman before, and knocked flat. He thought Amber had cut out his heart, but he realized tonight that he was becoming a whole man again. When he looked at

Emily, there wasn't a numb bone, muscle, sinew, organ or nerve in his body.

At the door, she pivoted and slanted him a mischievous look. "Are we going, or are you just going to stare all night, cowboy?"

Six

Thankful for the darkness, Zach caught up with Emily outside, carrying the shotgun he had retrieved from his gun rack. "Sorry to keep you waiting. I wanted to bring this."

"Is a weapon necessary?"

"I just want it available. I'll keep it in my truck."

She nodded, and they strode across the yard in silence while he inhaled her perfume and fought the urge to reach for her. At the pickup, he loaded the gun and placed it beneath the seat. "It won't be any use in an emergency if it's not loaded."

As he drove away from the ranch, Zach tried to get his body under control. He tried to think of the ranch, of cows, of horses, of anything except the woman beside him whose exotic perfume was a taunting reminder.

"If someone saw Amber last week in this bar, she must still be in this area."

"Who knows with your sister," he said. His voice was raspy and he could barely think about Amber or his destination. He cast quick glances at Emily and breathed deeply as if he were running full tilt up a mountainside. The woman was like a raging fire and he was getting singed just sitting in the car with her. He wanted to sink his hands into that mass of wild hair. He wanted to peel away the tight T-shirt, cup those full breasts in his hands, and stroke the nipples that only minutes earlier had tightened beneath his scrutiny.

He gripped the steering wheel until his knuckles hurt, and he ground his jaw closed, trying to keep his attention straight ahead. Instead, he glanced at her.

She's my ex-sister-in-law, he told himself silently, trying to remember all that meant. Off-limits. Do not touch. Forget that he enjoyed her company. Forget that the kids had taken to her as if they had known her always. Forget how she played with them and hugged Rebecca and picked her up. Forget the sexy lady!

"Nessie said Quint told her this was a tough bar."

"It is."

"Quint looks tough enough for any bar. For that matter, you do, too. Especially after last night." Emily glanced at Zach, who sat with his shoulders set, his hands on the wheel, staring straight ahead. She wondered whether he was angry at the thought of finding Amber.

"Nessie said you've helped Quint, too. There should be more like you. I wouldn't see so many unhappy people."

"My dad raised all of us to do whatever we can to help others," Zach said, keeping his attention on the road. He seemed more tense, and she noticed a muscle working in his jaw.

"You must have a nice father."

"He's great. He's a hard worker who had a hard life, but he always extends a helping hand to those who need it. He doesn't have a college education and when he was twenty, he worked at an oil refinery down in south Texas. There was an explosion and he was burned badly and pinned beneath some equipment. A man went in to get him and there was a second explosion. The guy stuck with my dad and got him out of there. He saved my dad's life when a lot of men died that day. My dad never forgot what that guy did for him, so when we were growing up, Dad taught us to help others. Dad was always bringing strangers home to dinner and giving them jobs.''

"That might not be safe to do nowadays.''

"No, probably not, but he was a pretty good judge of character. In all those years, we only had one bad incident and Dad sent that guy running like crazy.''

"You're lucky, Zach, to have a father like him,'' she said.

"He left that job and never could get health insurance after that. He bought a little bit of land and then a little more and made a go of it. Now he's got a good ranch, but his health isn't good and his medical bills are terrific.''

"I saw medical bills on your desk today. They're your father's, aren't they?''

"Yeah. He's had two heart attacks. I'm trying to take care of his medical bills for him. Alissa helps with them, too. Sean will help him with the ranch.''

Zach knew he was rambling, but he was barely aware of what he was saying; his thoughts were still on Emily. He didn't want to take her to a bar. Every man in the place would want to dance with her or talk to her. What he really wanted was to pull off to the side of the road, take her into his arms and kiss her senseless. He wanted her in his arms to fill the emptiness—the aching void—in himself.

"You don't want to do this tonight, do you?''

"No,'' he answered, startled because that was exactly what was on his mind. "I don't want to, but we need to check out the rumor, and this may be something I can do better than Nunez. God knows, you'll get any man there to talk to *you*.''

"I'm sorry if I'm dredging up bad memories for you,'' she said quietly.

The lady didn't understand that it wasn't bad memories

that had him tied into knots. And at this point, he didn't think he should inform her that she herself was making his pulse race and his hands sweat and his heart do its own Indy 500.

They sped through the darkness and Zach kept his attention glued to the stretch of gray highway zipping beneath them. Emily leaned back against the seat, worried about him. She was sorry for the trouble she had brought into his life. If only she could find Amber tonight. But at the thought of going home to Chicago, pain stabbed her. The past twenty-four hours had been wonderful—a special time that seemed far longer than the mere hours it actually had been.

It had been a moment in her life that would forever be etched in her memory, and her heart. She already loved her niece and nephew. She glanced at Zach. What did she feel for their father?

She knew she couldn't pursue the answer to that question. He was never going to be a permanent part of her life, and she should be aware that she would soon have to say goodbye. She would see him again because of the children, but she couldn't be part of his life in any way other than as their aunt—and his ex-sister-in-law. The sister of an ex-wife who'd hurt him terribly.

Unpredictable Amber could at any time, change her mind and step back into Zach's life. If, as Emily suspected, Amber had dumped Husband Number Three, Amber's disappearance could be a grand ploy to get Zach's attention and sympathy, and to move back. Her sister could be devious when she set her mind to it. Emily sighed, knowing she needed to get back to Chicago as quickly as possible.

"Why the big sigh?" he asked in a husky voice that showed he was battling his emotions.

"I was thinking about my job and home," she said, surprised that he had noticed.

He glanced at her and then back at the road.

"I still say, you should go home and let Nunez handle this."

"In another day or two, I will. If I'm an inconvenience for you—"

"No, you're not a damned inconvenience," he said tightly. She closed her mouth, wondering again if thoughts of finding Amber were tearing at him.

They rode in a tense silence until she saw the bar nestled back in the tall pines off the highway. Red neon splashed over the dirt lot filled with bikes and pickups. When Zach turned into the lot, she could hear the blare of country music. The place was made of pine logs with a tin roof that sloped out over a porch. Pine railing circled the porch and posts supported the roof. A flashing sign in the window advertised beer. The door was open revealing a dark interior.

Zach parked and held out the keys to the truck. "Take these. If there's a fight, run for the truck and lock yourself in."

"And abandon you?"

"I'll take care of myself and I can do it better if I don't have to worry about where you are and who has you."

"Sure," she said, taking the keys and jamming them into her jeans pocket.

"Here we go. I hope I get home in one piece, Chicago."

"If it's that rough, shouldn't we leave this for the sheriff?"

Zach grinned as they crossed the porch. "Hell, no. I wouldn't miss getting to dance with you for a dozen bare-knuckle fights."

They stepped inside and Zach paused, letting his eyes adjust to the darkness. Beneath a cloud of smoke, couples circled the dance floor as a CD blared out country music. He was relieved to see that about a fourth of the customers were couples. He had been in the place when there were only a few women and hordes of ornery men, but on dance nights, he knew, the bar drew more couples. He saw heads turn in their direction. Only it wasn't him they were staring at.

He slid his arm across Emily's shoulders possessively and pulled her against him. Perfume assailed him, and he was aware of the contact of his shoulders brushing her shoulder, his hip brushing hers, as he threaded among the other patrons and toward the back. Men whistled, and he heard catcalls as they passed a pool table near the front door.

"I hope they don't have to haul me away from here in an ambulance. Remember, when trouble starts, you run for the pickup."

"Yes, sir!" she snapped and he looked down to see a mischievous glint in her eyes. The woman had been nothing but trouble since he spotted big eyes peering into his kitchen window and saw her duck down out of sight. So why was his heart pounding like a jackhammer every time he looked at her or got close to her?

He spotted three empty tables, one close to the back wall. He led Emily toward it, moving among men who were staring openly at her.

"Hi, Zach. Out again?" a tall sandy-haired cowboy said, approaching them and staring at Emily.

"Hi, Ed," he answered, giving the cowboy a look that stopped him dead. "Meet Emily. Emily, this is Ed," he said, moving on quickly. He greeted people he knew, introducing Emily as they pushed through the crowd, giving the same hard look to every man he passed.

When they reached the table, he pulled out a chair and sat with his back to the wall so he had a good view of the place.

A man appeared before them instantly, smiling at Emily. "Hi. What'll you have?"

Zach ordered two beers before Emily could open her mouth. As soon as the waiter left them, Zach stood and reached down to take her hand. "Let's dance. If we sit, someone else will be asking you to dance."

He led her to the dance floor, pushed his hat squarely on his head and turned to face her. "Ever done the two-step?"

She nodded. "Yes, but I don't drink beer—which you ordered."

"You don't have to drink it, just keep it on the table. This place won't have soda pop."

"For a place with such a tough reputation, you sure know a lot of people here."

"I live in an area where the population is thin. Everyone knows everyone."

He began to dance, and she followed him easily, aware of his hand on her waist, his other hand holding hers. A dark eyebrow arched as he watched her. "I thought you said you don't date. You didn't learn how to two-step sitting home alone."

She smiled at him. "I don't date enough for it to be significant—but of course I've dated."

"I'll bet you have. You dance like you've been doing this all your life."

"I like to dance."

He moved with her in perfect unison, as if the two of them had danced together before. He forgot everyone else, feeling himself drowning in her big green eyes, which widened and focused on him intently. She was a feather to hold: warm, soft, sweet-smelling. All woman. She was all the things that he admired—responsible, intelligent, spirited. And she turned him on like a million megavolts. He felt as if he was reminding himself on the half-hour now how off-limits she was to him. Was he being foolish? The instant he asked himself the question, he knew his answer. With the exception of his children, and in spite of all the good things about Emily, he couldn't get involved.

The number stopped, then another started and he moved right into it with her, still watching her and feeling his body tighten in response. His hand was on her waist, and he could feel her hips sway as she danced. He could feel her warm bare skin just above her jeans where the shirt ended.

Every other guy that danced with her was going to feel the same thing. The thought made Zach want to hold her tightly, dance a few more times and then whisk her home. He didn't want another guy dancing with her or looking at her or touching her.

Shocked at the intensity of his feelings, he wondered at himself. He had never been that uptight about a woman before. Emily brought out all kinds of feelings in him that amazed him and made him feel as if he didn't know himself. He had thought he was numb to females. So much for that one. He didn't know he could possibly be jealous. Surprise, surprise. And the rest—the way she turned him on, the way he enjoyed her, and the way her presence filled the house with warmth—that was what had shaken him up most of all.

Well, maybe not *most* of all. He thought about the wild kisses they had shared this morning.

Trying to tear his gaze from hers and his thoughts from such memories, he turned his head. He ought to keep the ranch, the kids, on his mind. His life was consumed with skinned knees, drippy noses, cows, horses, medical bills and ranch expenses. He had no business losing his reason and purpose over a big-eyed city girl who would be in his life only days.

But what a joy today had been! The aching loneliness had vanished, an easy companionship was established, and an excitement was steadily building.

Forget her, he told himself silently.

"If we keep dancing with each other, you're not going to learn anything about Amber, and I won't either," she said.

"Yeah, I know."

"So shouldn't we move away from each other?"

He looked into her eyes, and she inhaled deeply. He dropped his gaze as the T-shirt stretched even more tautly over her breasts. He wanted to groan. "Yeah, Chicago, we should move away from each other, but damned if I want to.'' She blinked as if startled and mystified by his answer. If she only knew what she was doing to him, moving with the grace of a willow branch in the breeze, yet looking tempting enough to set a man on fire.

The music stopped and a stranger appeared instantly at her side.

''Hi. Can I have the next dance?'' Without waiting for an answer, he stepped between Zach and Emily.

Zach clenched his fists, curbed his impulse to claim her, and turned around to find Aggie Wilson staring at him. She smiled. ''Hi, Zach. See you're back in circulation.''

''Yep. Want to dance, Aggie?''

The petite blonde smiled and moved into his arms. As he began to dance, he glanced across the room and saw Emily. She was smiling, moving with a sexy sway to her hips. It took an effort to force his attention back to Aggie.

''Glad you're out again.''

''Actually, I'm out looking for Amber. You haven't seen her lately, have you?''

''No. I didn't think you two ever wanted to see each other again. Was I wrong?''

''That's her sister who's with me. She's searching for Amber and Amber's been seen around here. Her sister is worried about her.''

Aggie laughed. ''She might as well worry about a tigress. That woman can take care of herself.''

''Yeah, I know. But if you hear anything, let me know.''

''Sure. Still, you're out. It ought to feel good. And if you'd go out with someone besides your sister-in-law—*ex*-sister-in-law—it would feel even better,'' she said in a soft voice, moving closer to him.

''I can't leave the kids much. They're at a cute age now.'' As he continued talking about his children, he looked over Aggie's head and spotted Emily, watched her dance. When the dance finished, another man asked Aggie to dance and Zach returned to their table to pick up his beer. After taking a long drink, he crossed the room to the bar, where he made an excuse to talk to the man beside him. Later he talked to the bartender, a stocky blonde.

"Yeah, I remember her coming in here. I don't know the guy, but no one is going to forget that woman."

"If you hear anything about them, I'd like to know," Zach said, pulling out a business card and slipping bills with it.

"Thanks, mister."

Slowly, Zach worked his way along the bar, moving to the pool table, asking first one person and then another about Amber. He danced with a tall black-haired woman named Josey Garza. When the dance ended, he was only a few feet from Emily. A cowboy asked Josey to dance and Zach stepped away quickly, seeing two men headed toward Emily.

"I get this dance, Chicago."

"Sure thing, cowboy." The music started and she danced with him, her eyes meeting his.

"Having fun?" he asked.

"I am now," she answered, and his pulse jumped.

"Learn anything?"

She nodded. "See the guy in the bright red shirt?" She looked over the crowd. "He's dancing with a tall blonde."

Zach spotted the man she was referring to, and nodded.

"He remembers dancing with Amber. And he said the guy she was with might work for a man named Henshaw."

"Bingo! I've heard of Craig Henshaw. We can check that out tomorrow."

"He wasn't certain. There's another guy who remembered her. He's in a plaid shirt and he's a little bald, with black whiskers on his face. I don't see him now. He didn't know the guy she was with, either, but he said she was having a good time."

"When *hasn't* Amber had a good time?" he snapped. Then he looked at Emily, every thought of Amber rushing from his mind. He watched the play of emotions on her face as she moved in step with him. Erotic fantasies began to play in his mind and he blocked out everyone else in the room. "We do all right together," he whispered softly.

"It's too soon to tell."

"Like hell it is. There hasn't been a misstep."

Emily's pulse raced with the suspicion that he wasn't just talking about dancing.

"Then you're a lot more certain about what you're doing than I am."

"Just follow your heart, Chicago," he said quietly and tightened his arm, pulling her closer to him. He was flirting with her, and she was responding. It was a dangerous thing to do. Everything about him was dangerous to her peace of mind, her heart, her well-being. Yet she would always be tied to him by the children—her little niece and nephew that she would never again ignore. Her life in Chicago was going to be incredibly lonely when she returned. How long would it take to forget him? She wondered whether she ever would.

The minute the dance was over, another man asked for her hand. Zach returned to the bar, talking to strangers, asking questions, until he came to a cowboy he had ridden with in rodeos.

"Dusty, have you seen Amber lately? I'm looking for her."

"I don't know why you're looking for her. That's a babe you brought here tonight. Mind if I dance with her?"

"No," Zach lied. He minded like hell, particularly when it was someone he had already questioned and who would no longer be helpful for Emily to talk to. "She's Amber's sister."

"The hell you say." Dusty grinned. "What a family! And she's your sister-in-law. You brought a relative tonight."

Zach wanted to swear and shout that the woman was not related to him, that she was his date, and that everyone should keep their hands off. But he knew that was ridiculous.

Dusty shifted, crossing his arms over his chest. "I've seen Amber."

Zach turned to stare at the cowboy, who wore a battered gray hat and a plaid shirt. "Where did you see her? And when?"

"Here in this bar about three nights ago," he answered without taking his eyes off the dancers.

"Who was she with?"

"I don't know the guy. He's a stranger to me, but it sure 'nuff was Amber. No mistaking that woman. You can really pick 'em, Zach. I'm going to ask your sister-in-law to dance, pardner.' Dusty drained his beer, set the empty on the bar and crossed the room.

So far, several men had seen Amber in the past week. And the man she was with might work for Craig Henshaw. From all reports, she was healthy, probably doing what she wanted. So now Emily would pack up and go back to Chicago.

Zach hurt, and he hated the pain. He shouldn't care. He hadn't known Emily long enough to care. He watched the willowy redhead moving around the dance floor. Why did being with her seem so incredibly right?

Annoyed with himself, he picked up his beer and began searching the crowd for the guy in the red shirt who might know the man Amber had been with.

Emily moved in time to the music. She liked to dance, but she wanted it to be with Zach. Wasn't he going to dance with her again tonight? She smiled at the cowboy leading her around the floor, trying to listen to what he was saying. She had been flirted with enough for one night. A few of the guys were really nice, a few came on too strong and were obnoxious, but most of them were a blur. There was only one man she was aware of.

She turned and looked across the barroom, seeing him with his hat pushed to the back of his head as he leaned over the pool table. What was it about Zach that made her pulse leap? She had met at least twenty men tonight and none of them had had the least effect on her. They flirted and they were more interested in dating her than was Zach—yet it meant nothing.

She didn't *want* Zach to be special. He couldn't be. She didn't want a magical chemistry—not with that cowboy.

Her thoughts reeling, she concentrated instead on her partner. "I'm here looking for my sister, Amber Durham, only now it's Amber Morales." For all Emily knew, it was no longer Morales, either.

"Nope, I haven't seen Amber in a long time," the short, thickset cowboy answered.

As soon as the dance ended, another man moved in. "Let's dance," he said, taking her firmly in his arms, pulling her too close. He was as tall as Zach, barrel-chested and brawny. He wore a tank top that revealed powerful muscles and a chest covered in thick black hair.

"I'm Buck Dayton. I haven't seen you before."

"I'm Emily Stockton. I'm here looking for my sister, Amber Durham."

"I don't know her," he said. Emily tried to put more space between them, but his arm tightened and he held her close. He smelled like sweat and beer and tobacco, and she wanted away from him. His blue eyes undressed her every time he looked at her, and she felt a knot of revulsion forming.

"I'm here with Zach Durham. Amber is his ex-wife."

"Sorry, baby, but I don't know any of them. But I know you now and want to know you better. Where you been hiding yourself?"

"I live in Chicago."

"Hell of a ways from here. Where you staying?"

"I'm staying with Zach."

"The brother-in-law." To Emily's relief, the music ended.

"Thanks. I want to go freshen up."

"Yeah. I'll get you through the crowd." They moved from the dance floor and as they approached the side of the room, Buck's hand closed on her arm. "Have you ever ridden a bike?"

"No, I haven't."

"Come here and let me show you mine. I've got the damn best bike, baby. I can give you a ride you won't ever forget."

They were halfway across the room when he pulled her toward the front door. Emily resisted, but her strength was no match for his. "Thanks, no."

"Come on, baby," he coaxed.

"No, I'm not going with you. Let go of me."

He grinned. "Six bits says you are going with me. You'll be glad. Lighten up, babe. Come on." He pulled her toward the door again. Anger flooded her.

She stomped her heel on his boot, but he merely widened his grin. She didn't want to make a scene or cause a fight, but she wasn't leaving the bar with the man. She began dragging her heels, trying to get free and avoid trouble, but they were narrowing the distance to the door.

"Let go of me!" she ordered in a low voice.

"Naw, baby. Not tonight. You're a doll and we—"

"Take your hands off my woman."

Zach's voice was quiet, yet it carried as clearly as if it had been a shout. Her heart missed a beat and she whirled around.

Zach blocked the way to the door. He stood with his feet apart, his fists on his hips and the look in his eye should have been warning enough. A chill ran down her spine at the coldness in his eyes, but his words tumbled in her mind like flower petals spilling in summer sunshine. *My woman.*

Warmth flooded her as she stared at him. *His woman.* She wanted to be exactly that. And she knew how dangerous it was to want to be part of his life. That wasn't what he wanted; he was merely protecting her. He hadn't meant what he said except as a way to get her out of the bar and safely home.

Men moved out of the way. For an instant, no one spoke.

Then Buck tightened his grip on her arm. "The hell she is. You ain't danced with her since you got here."

She gave a twist and broke free from him, rushing toward Zach. He clenched his fists and didn't take his eyes from Buck. She glanced over her shoulder to see Buck raising his fists and she knew they were going to fight.

"Let's go," she urged Zach.

"Get out of here," he answered without looking at her. Buck rushed him, and Zach stepped out of his way, swinging his fist.

She remembered the pickup and the keys in her pocket and ran for the door just as she heard someone crash into a table behind her. Men yelled, glass shattered, wood smashed. A brawl was on.

Cool night air enveloped her while her heart raced. Buck was a good sixty pounds heavier than Zach, she was sure. And he might have friends back there. Her heart thudded, and her hands shook. She heard the splintering of glass, and glanced around to see a man fly through one of the windows. He hit the porch railing, fell to the ground and lay still.

She yanked open the door of the pickup and grabbed the shotgun, then raced back to the bar.

Emily stepped through the door, momentarily stunned by the melee. Men were tossing bottles, slugging each other. She couldn't spot Zach.

She raised the shotgun and pumped it, and at the double clicks the men closest to her froze. She aimed at the ceiling and fired.

Seven

The blast was deafening and every man in the room froze. Emily lowered the shotgun to level it straight in front of her.

Her gaze flitted over the scene, some men standing and others sprawled about the room. Then she spotted a lanky figure stretched on the floor. Zach raised his head, shook it, and stood. Blood streamed from a cut on his temple; his cheek was scraped, his mouth was bleeding. His T-shirt was half torn away and blood speckled his clothing. As he faced her, a grin lifted one corner of his mouth in a lopsided smile.

"I think my woman and I will go home now," he said, stumbling as he stood, then walking with a wobbly step. He paused to scoop up his battered hat, and staggered over to her, taking the shotgun from her and backing out the door with the gun leveled at the room. As soon as they crossed the porch steps, he whooped and laughed.

"I don't know what you think is funny," Emily snapped.

She was shaking, afraid they would be jumped before they could get to the pickup. At the same time his words kept running through her mind, over and over. *My woman and I*... "I'm shaking so much I can barely walk," she added. "And you look like a truck hit you."

"Let's get the hell out of here." He grabbed her arm.

"Want me to drive?" she asked.

"No, I can." They raced to the pickup, and she climbed inside while he went around to ease behind the wheel. He locked the doors and placed the shotgun on the rack, then turned to start the ignition. They sped onto the highway and headed toward the ranch.

"Zach, you're bleeding badly. Shouldn't you get those cuts sewed up?"

He laughed again and whipped the pickup to the side of the road.

"What are you doing?"

After cutting the lights and the motor, he turned to her. Bright moonlight made it easy to see him as he fished for a handkerchief. He wiped blood off his mouth, and held the handkerchief to his bleeding temple while he tangled his other hand in her hair.

"You're something else, Emily Stockton! Where did you learn to handle a shotgun?"

Startled by this exuberant side to him that she hadn't seen before, Emily answered, "I grew up in a tough neighborhood with a thief for a father, remember? He kept a shotgun and one time after he went to prison, a guy broke into the apartment and attacked my mother. I got the shotgun and he ran. I realized I better learn how to use the thing because the next time the guy might not run."

Zach grinned. "I will never forget looking up and seeing you standing there like an avenging angel with that shotgun in your hand. That was worth getting hit. I'll bet no one has moved yet. You're amazing, lady."

"That's ridicul—"

His hand tightened behind her head, and he pulled her

to him. His mouth came down on hers hard in a hungry, possessive kiss that sent a flash of fire down to her toes. The world vanished and only Zach existed. She knew the kiss must be hurting him—but then she forgot about his pain.

His lips were demanding, eager. The exuberance he had shown carried over into his kiss. Warning bells went off in her mind, but they were dim, unheeded. She had never been kissed this way in her life. His tongue stroked hers and it was not a kiss of seduction, but a kiss of discovery and challenge.

She wound her hands behind his neck and returned his kiss while sensations zinged in her body and heat built in her. She had taken risks before and she would take risks now because this was a once in a lifetime kind of kiss. Her tongue flicked over his, stroking and tasting.

Tightening his arms around her, Zach kissed her wildly. What a woman she was! No strait-laced, do-good city slicker. The woman was gutsy, feisty and sexy. She had taken on a bar of rough men, and the look in her eyes had carried as much threat as the shotgun in her hands.

A car whipped past them, and a horn blared.

"Zach." Leaning back, Emily opened her eyes to look at him. She was breathless, stunned from his kisses. "Shouldn't we get a move on before someone comes after us?"

His dark eyes were devastating as he stared at her with a need that she could see even in the moonlight. "Yeah," he answered gruffly and inhaled deeply. Tossing down his blood-soaked handkerchief, he yanked off what was left of his shirt and swiped with it at the blood on his temple. He started the pickup and swung back onto the highway to speed into the darkness.

Silence enveloped them. But Emily's lips tingled and her body was on fire. Why did kisses have to be so spectacular with this man? Why was he the one whose company she enjoyed constantly?

When they finally turned onto the ranch road, the tenseness in her grew. She was going back to his house. Nessie would leave. The children were asleep. She would be alone with Zach.

He parked by the back gate and as soon as they entered the house, he switched off the alarm. "Nessie, we're home."

Nessie strolled into the kitchen with her book under her arm. When she saw them, her mouth dropped open. "Oh, my gosh! It was worse than I thought it would be."

Zach grinned and pointed at Emily. "She saved me."

"No kidding!"

"I just got the shotgun," Emily said, embarrassed, still shaken by the incident and the kisses that had followed.

"And brought that whole bar to a standstill," he said, laughing.

"Looks like you should have gone to the emergency room and gotten sewed up."

"I told you we should have done that," Emily added. "Let me take you now."

"I'm taking myself to a shower and I'll be fine."

"Men!" Nessie threw up her hands and crossed the room to the door. She squinted her eyes, looking at Emily. "I'll bet you had a good time."

"I had a busy time," she answered, blushing, aware of Zach in her peripheral vision grinning at her.

"Danced her damned toes off and saved my butt," he said, pulling out his billfold and handing bills to Nessie. "Thanks for coming up and staying with the kids."

"You're welcome. You should have taken Quint and some of the guys with you."

"I'm okay."

"My sister is in the area. We talked to several men who've seen her this week," Emily added.

Nessie's dark eyebrows arched. "You think she's all right then?"

Emily and Zach looked at each other, and Emily nodded.

"If she was out dancing, I imagine she is fine. But I'd still like to talk to her before I go home."

"Oh, Emily, you had two phone calls. One said to call back no matter how late, and the other said to call the office tomorrow." Nessie crossed to the phone and tore paper off a pad to hand to Emily.

"Thanks."

"Well, I'll run. 'Night." Nessie went out the door, and Emily hurried after her.

"Nessie." Emily saw a tall figure walking slowly toward the back gate and recognized Quint, who had come up to meet Nessie. "Thanks for helping me get ready."

"Sure. I hope you had some fun."

"I did," she answered softly, remembering how it had felt to dance in Zach's arms. After a final good-night, she went inside, while Zach locked up and set the alarm.

"I'm washing up. I want a beer. What would you like?"

"Iced tea sounds good, but I'll get it. If you don't get some bandages, you're going to be dripping blood on the floor."

"Sure, Mom," he said lightly and brushed a kiss on the tip of her nose. She made a face in return. He grinned as he got his beer and the pitcher of tea from the refrigerator.

Don't get too much fun to be with, she thought as she watched him. For the first time, she noticed a deep slash across his right shoulder. His jeans showed a crimson stain on his upper thigh.

She gasped at the deep, ugly wounds. "Zach, you're cut!"

"There were a few knives in the place. I had my knife strapped in my boot, but I didn't get it out."

"You've got two bad cuts—one on your back and one on your leg." He shot her a look and she threw up her hands. "All right, Mr. Macho. Enjoy your battle wounds." He grinned and reached for a glass. She hurried to his side.

"I'll do that," she said, taking the pitcher from him.

"Thanks." She watched him stride from the room, her

pulse racing just from being near him. She was still shaken from the bar fight—and from his kisses on the way home. She had thought their kisses that morning had been earth-shaking, but the ones tonight were even more devastating.

Refusing to let her errant thoughts roam any further, instead she focused on the reality of the situation. Amber was somewhere nearby. She'd been dancing at that bar, so she had to be all right. Emily knew she should try to find her sister tomorrow and then go home. Each day with Zach only fueled feelings she didn't want. They might be meaningless to him, but they meant something to her. One thing was certain—he wasn't numb. He reacted to their kisses swiftly and unmistakably, setting her aflame.

She fixed a glass of iced tea and took it to her room, where she heard the shower running. The image of Zach—muscled, bronzed, naked—flashed in mind. She tried to think about home and work. She called Meg and was still deep in conversation with her about a woman at the shelter when she heard a slight rap on the bathroom door. She stretched the phone cord and opened the door. Zach stood before her, dressed in a clean white T-shirt and jeans, his wet hair combed back from his face. He held a gauze pad against the cut on his temple. His mouth was swollen, one eye was turning dark and a dark bruise was showing on his jaw.

"I'm out," he whispered. "Come downstairs when you're off the phone."

She nodded and he left, closing the door behind him. As he turned away, she saw a circle of red on the back of his T-shirt where he was still bleeding.

Right now Zach needed her attention more than Meg. "Call Mason or Brian in the morning, Meg. They're our attorneys and they should know all this." Emily made some notes, cut short the call and said goodbye.

She replaced the receiver, kicked off her shoes, retrieved her glass of tea and went downstairs to find Zach. He stood leaning against the kitchen counter, drinking his beer with his feet crossed at the ankles. He was barefoot, still holding the gauze pad, now soaked and crimson—against his forehead.

"Zach, you're still bleeding. Do you want me to bandage that?"

"I can do it. I thought it would stop bleeding."

"Turn around."

He straightened and turned, glancing over his shoulder. "Oh, damn."

"You're bleeding badly," she said, looking at the red stain on his T-shirt and his jeans.

"All right. I'll need help with the one on my back. I can do my head."

"Trouble at work?" he asked as they climbed the stairs.

"A little. Meg Dodson is my assistant and she had some problems over a woman at the shelter. Our lawyers can handle it and Meg's already called the police. A woman who was a battered wife is being stalked and the guy has talked her parents into trying to get her back home through the courts. They're charging she's mentally incompetent, but she's not. We've got doctors we use and we have lawyers. They'll work it out."

In the bathroom, Zach got out gauze, antiseptic, tape and scissors. She watched while he put more antiseptic on the cut on his temple and began to bandage it. "If you'll sit down, I'll do that," she said, watching him struggle with a strip of gauze.

He moved to the side of the footed tub and sat down. Emily began to work, aware of—as she stood close beside him and touched him—of his eyes steadily on her. Her breasts were at his eye level, and once again she became aware of the skimpiness and tightness of her T-shirt.

She twisted, reaching behind her for tape while she held a gauze pad in place.

"What is this?" he asked. His warm fingers brushed her ribs, pushing the T-shirt up.

"What are you doing?"

"Damnation. I did this to you." He looked at the large bruise on her side.

"I'll recover," she said breathlessly, knowing he was holding the shirt high enough to see a fraction of her lacy bra.

"Have you got more bruises?"

"Maybe, but like you said, I'll be all right. I'm healing."

His dark eyes met hers as he slowly pulled the shirt back down, his fingers a caress on her bare skin. "I'm sorry."

"It was my fault, I suppose," she replied, hearing the huskiness in her voice and knowing that he must hear it, too. His hand lingered on her midriff, his fingers running back and forth along the top of her jeans. She tingled, aware of him and what he was doing. "You're going to have to turn around and take off your shirt so I can bandage your back."

He stood, yanked off his shirt and tossed it down. "Come in my room and I'll sit on the bed where you can reach my shoulder."

Gathering bandages and antiseptic, she followed him into the bedroom. When she had talked to him last night, she hadn't been able to focus on anything except Zach, but now she glanced around his masculine room. For a moment she remembered that Amber had lived here as his wife, and she felt a strange bitter twist inside. She tried not to pursue it, reminding herself that Amber was gone from Zach's life.

The four-poster double bed was unmade. Clothes and dusty boots were strewn about. This room, like the office, held a desk piled high with papers. There was a gun rack filled with rifles, a large, mahogany rocking chair, two large chests and mirrors along one wall.

Zach sat on the bed and she placed everything on a bedside table. "This looks like an old bed," she said, disconcerted and uncertain what she was babbling about. Her attention was on him—his muscled back, the pull of his tight jeans when he sat down, his long leg stretched out in front of him and the other leg doubled up on the bed.

"It was my granddad's. I had a water bed when I was married. I got rid of the damned thing and hauled this down from the attic. It's narrow, but it's okay for me." His voice was a deep rumble as he talked, and too easily she could imagine him stretched on the bed.

"It's really pretty," she said, glancing at the ornately carved posts and headboard.

Zach's tanned back was smooth, warm beneath her fingers. She held the bottle of antiseptic and a pad. "This is going to hurt."

"Get it done."

"I almost forgot. Mr. Macho." He gasped as she poured antiseptic on the cut.

"Damn, you don't have to dump the whole bottle on me."

"Stop whining."

He turned to grin at her and she caught her breath, her T-shirt stretching tautly across her breasts. Zach's gaze dropped. She felt as if he were touching her instead of merely looking at her.

"Turn around," she whispered.

He gave her a solemn look that was heated and more disturbing than when he'd been looking at her breasts. He turned his back to her and sat quietly.

"Your thigh is cut badly and bleeding enough to go through your jeans.

"Oh, damn it. I'll do it."

"You'll never reach it. Drop your jeans and I'll bandage it."

He grinned at her and she felt the flush that was already in her cheeks heat to fire.

"The lady says to drop my pants," he said in a husky, suggestive tone. "I'll guarantee you, I'm not about to argue." He turned his back to unfasten his jeans and let them fall below his knees.

She had been hot with embarrassment before. Now she was on fire, but with a different emotion. She looked at strong legs covered in short dark hair, and briefs that clung and outlined his round, firm bottom.

Zach's amusement vanished the moment he felt the brush of her fingers on the back of his thigh. His body responded and he was rock-hard, wanting to turn and pick her up and kiss her until she was responding as she had before. If he turned around, she would see exactly what effect she had on him. He wanted her in his bed, beneath him, her softness enveloping him.

He gasped and gritted his teeth as the antiseptic stung. "Hey!" Then her hands were brushing his leg again and he forgot the pain of his injury. Her hands were on the back of his thigh, her knuckles brushing his butt. He was aroused, aching with wanting her.

He remembered her dancing in his arms, seductively swaying and moving, her big green eyes pulling him into depths that felt as if he had waited forever to reach. Nearly every guy in the bar had wanted her. He had heard the damned whistles and catcalls and saw the looks she got. If she was aware of them, she never gave any indication and knowing Emily, she probably never guessed that they were directed at her.

She had looked sexy as hell tonight. And when that blast had gone off and he had raised his head, he couldn't believe his eyes. He had wanted to get up off the floor, haul her off into the bushes and take her. She had reacted coolly, bravely, and defiantly. And she looked all woman, enough to sizzle a man into fine ash. He loved her for it. The woman was amazing, looking so wide-eyed and helpless, yet as competent as they came—and sexier than most. So much more sexier. Or was it his reaction to her? Some special chemistry between them?

The thought staggered him. He wasn't ready for a relationship again. He would *never* be ready for an affair with Amber's sister. Or would he? Wasn't that what he had just been fantasizing about?

Forget she's Amber's sister, he told himself.

That was a frightening thing to do, because it wasn't the truth. How easy it would be. How easy to blind himself to her heritage. And when he tried, he wanted Emily in a way he had never before wanted a woman.

Her fingers flitted over his thigh and he had to grind his teeth and clench his fists to keep from turning and hauling her into his arms. Did she have any idea what she was doing to him, her fingers straying to the inside of his thigh as she secured the bandage she had made? She was damned close to touching him intimately. If she did, he wasn't sure about his control.

He felt a throbbing, and sweat formed on his neck even though he was standing still. What he felt for her went far beyond the mere physical. That was what terrified him. Had it been just physical, he could have coped better. But it was much more. The lady was warmhearted, intelligent, fun. And his desire for her was driving him to the brink.

"I'm finished," she said. Her voice was breathless, ragged, and he realized she was reacting to touching him. He bit back a groan, yanked up his jeans and buttoned them, then he stood and turned.

He watched her for a moment, rolling up a strip of gauze, her tongue caught between her teeth as she concentrated. Then he reached out to take the tape from her hands and toss it on the bed. She looked up at him and then her eyes widened, her pupils dilating. He pulled her toward him.

"Come here," he said in a husky voice. He wanted to tell her she was special, unique. He wanted to tell her how impressed he had been tonight with her courage. How much he had liked dancing with her. How great she looked. Instead, he couldn't utter a word. He drew her close, spreading his legs. He framed her face with his hands, sinking his fingers into her silky hair, feeling it curl over the backs of his hands and wrists and tickle his arms. He tilted her head up and leaned down to place his lips over hers, opening her mouth for his tongue.

With a sigh, she stepped closer. He felt twinges of pain

when they pressed their bodies together, and when his lips touched hers. He didn't care. In seconds, he forgot the pain. Longing and hot desire took its place. He was tossing aside wisdom and all the promises he had made to himself. At this moment, though, he didn't care that she was Amber's sister. He didn't care about all the sensible decisions he had made. Emily was in his arms, the way she should be.

She thrust her hips against him, tightened her arms around his neck and returned his kisses with passion. She moaned softly, and he shook with need. He shifted slightly, sliding his hands along her warm, bare midriff. His fingers drifted up over soft curves to unclasp her flimsy bra. He released her, caught the T-shirt in his hands and pulled it over her head.

She gazed at him with a look that made his blood thunder through his veins, and he cupped her breasts in his hands. The warmth and softness shook him and he bent, taking a taut nipple in his mouth and flicking it with his tongue.

He felt her hands tangling in his hair, heard her moan of pleasure as he sucked and licked the rosy tip, then moved to the other breast.

She was beautiful, perfect. Trembling beneath his touch, she responded wildly, her hands sliding over his chest, down to his thighs. He groaned.

"Zach."

He wasn't sure he heard his name, but he felt the faint push against his shoulders. She twisted, stepped away and scooped up her T-shirt to hold it in front of her, but he could still see the curves of her lush breasts on either side. She gasped for breath and her face was flushed, her mouth red from his kisses.

"We're not ready for this. Neither one of us. You don't really want a relationship with me, and I don't want one with you—and we both know why. She might as well be in the room between us."

He took a deep breath and, clenched his fists, shaking. He tried to control the urge to close the distance between them and put a swift end to her protests. Instead, he remained immobile, wanting her. His emotions churned, and questions flew through his mind. What did he really want? What could he forget?

He had made a dreadful mistake once before in his life. He didn't want to make another one now.

Emily turned for the bathroom, and he looked at her slender back. He wanted her in a way he couldn't ever remember wanting a woman before. He had *wanted* women before—he'd wanted Amber, been tied in knots about her—but it had always been physical.

"Emily," he called as the door closed behind her. When he heard a muffled reply, he continued, "come downstairs and bring your tea."

He yanked on a clean T-shirt, switched off the lights and went downstairs. He found his beer, left the hall light on and sat in the semidarkness of the family room. He was beginning to wonder whether she would come downstairs at all, when he heard her moving in the hall.

"I'm in here," he said.

She crossed the room and he stood. "Come sit over here."

She sat on the opposite end of the sofa from him. She was wearing his chambray shirt, which hung to her knees, and her jeans and sneakers. Her hair was brushed and fastened with a clip behind her head, and her face was scrubbed, the makeup gone. He didn't care. His pulse raced at the sight of her. Again he felt his body heating and he fought the urge to reach for her.

"I've been thinking about Amber. No one knows the man she was with, but there are four people who remember seeing her this past week. She's in this area and she must be all right. I have a description of the guy she was with."

"I do, too. And she was definitely with him. She came with him, danced with him, and left with him."

"Okay, let's match descriptions—wait a minute, don't say anything." He left and returned with pencils and paper.

"Let's write down what we were told so we don't influence each other. Get down everything you remember, then we can compare what we learned. If I can take Nunez a good description, he can find the guy, or may even recognize who the guy is. Tomorrow we can go out to Henshaw's and ask about Amber."

Emily took a piece of paper and a pencil, and Zach watched as, head bent, she jotted down what she remembered. Her profile was backlighted by the hall light and Zach noticed her straight nose, her high cheekbones, her full, incredibly soft mouth. He wanted to remove the clip from her hair, kiss the nape of her neck and pull her onto his lap.

Tomorrow or the next day, she would find Amber and then Emily would go back to Chicago. And he knew that even if Amber and Emily's bloodlines didn't stand between them, her responsible job and big-city life would. A woman like Emily—accustomed to daily responsibilities, the fast pace of urban life—would hate it as much as her sister had. He had already married one woman who had never fit into his life. Now here he was, falling for another who didn't fit his life-style—and would never want to.

"Do you like to ride, Chicago?" he asked as he made some notes himself.

Her head came up and she looked at him. "Ride? What?"

"Ride a horse?" he answered with amusement.

"I have never ridden a horse."

"Want to try?"

"When? I don't know whether I can."

"You can. Even Rebecca can ride one. In the morning we could take the kids out for a ride."

"Both children ride horses?"

"Rebecca can ride by herself. I usually take Jason on the horse with me."

"Do they like that?"

"Love it. Want to go?"

Emily thought about riding with him. She loved the children and wanted to spend more time with them before she returned to Chicago. And she wanted to be with their daddy—badly.

"I really should see about Amber—and then get back to Chicago, Zach," she said quietly, knowing that was the wisest answer. "But I'll think about it," she added anyway.

"Sure," Zach said stiffly. Then, abruptly, he said, "Let's compare notes." He moved beside her, knowing there was no need to sit so close. Yet if she noticed, she didn't say anything.

"He's thin, weathered, tanned, blue-eyed, and tall."

"That's pretty much what I've got," Zach said. "And the description fits half the men in the next three counties. He smoked, wore nondescript clothing—jeans, the usual."

"He drove away in a red pickup."

"There's something," Zach said, looking at her notes. "Red pickup. That will narrow it down to several hundred in the area. Good."

"He wore a ring on his finger and a gold chain around his neck."

"Hey, you got more out of them than I did—which is no surprise. The men I talked to didn't notice the jewelry. I'll take what we have to Nunez tomorrow."

Zach shifted, facing her with his knee bent on the sofa. While he talked, his fingers played over her knee lightly, feeling the soft material of her jeans, the warmth of the skin beneath.

Emily was conscious of his fingers touching her lightly while they talked. Their conversation shifted from the evening, to the ranch and his grandfather, to her job and her life in Chicago.

As they talked, he turned and moved closer. His hand drifted across her shoulder, along her arm. She tingled, each touch a reminder of their kisses. They talked until four in the morning. When they finally ventured upstairs for bed, Zach kissed her until Emily told him to stop. With both of them gasping for breath, she went to her room and closed the door.

At dawn the next morning, they rode with the children, and she felt a sense of joy and peace she had never before known. But as they turned back to the barn, the euphoria changed to a painful regret. All too soon she would leave for Chicago. How empty the long drive back would be! Her gaze went to the tall cowboy riding ahead of her through the stand of pines. He sat straight, his hat squarely on his head, his arm around Jason. Emily's heart raced just watching him ride.

Two hours later, Zach turned the pickup along a rutted road, crossed a cattle guard and wound along a valley surrounded by mountains. "It's beautiful here," Emily remarked, watching the silvery glitter of aspen leaves fluttering in the breeze.

"I think so—the most beautiful place on earth. But I'll bet you think it's a lot prettier in Chicago."

"That's like comparing apples and skis. They're entirely different."

"Yeah," he said, becoming silent. She saw the firm set to his jaw and wondered what was running through his mind. His morning cheer had faded, transforming to a tight-lipped silence. Harshness returned to his expression. Was he getting tense over the prospect of finding Amber? Did he still love Amber?

At the Henshaw ranch they crossed a creek. In a nearby pasture, cattle grazed, and Emily saw a ranch house in the distance. Within minutes they came to the barns where a man was chopping wood.

"Just a sec," Zach said and got out, striding to the man who pushed back his hat and straightened up. She couldn't hear them, but could see them talking. The man pointed, and Zach nodded before returning to the pickup.

"Henshaw is putting in a new stock tank about a mile down the road."

"Amber can't be staying in a bunkhouse."

"No, but some of the men have houses, or he could work here and live elsewhere." Zach was silent until they spotted men and trucks in a pasture. "There's Henshaw."

They slowed and turned, bouncing over rough ground as Zach drove to the tank where three men were working. One stood and dropped his tools, then walked toward the pickup.

"Come with me," Zach said. "I might need you to bat your big eyes at him. Some of these guys are pretty close-mouthed about the men who work for them."

Zach climbed out of the pickup and Emily stepped down to join him. A beefy man with weathered skin strode to meet them. He wore a battered gray hat pushed back to reveal brown hair. His jaw was covered in brown stubble, and his clothes were covered in dust.

"Mr. Henshaw," Zach said, extending his hand. "I'm Zach Durham and this is Emily Stockton."

"Yeah, I remember you. Morning, ma'am," he said politely to Emily.

"Good morning." Emily flashed him a smile, while Zach stood close beside her without touching her.

"Miss Stockton is here from Chicago. She's searching for her sister and we heard she was with a man who might work for you."

Blue eyes studied Zach, and Emily could feel the reluctance in Craig Henshaw. "He do that to you?" he asked, looking at Zach's injuries.

"No. That's from a fight at the Full Moon Bar last night. That's not why I'm hunting him. It's just so Emily can find her sister."

Henshaw nodded as if satisfied with the answer. "Know the man's name you're searching for?"

"No, we don't. No one seems to know him. Several men gave us a description and said Emily's sister was with him. Her sister is my ex-wife. She's a very beautiful woman. The man has dark hair—"

"His name is Corky Powell," Henshaw interrupted. "She *is* a beautiful woman. And you might have come too late to see them. Corky quit and they left, or are leaving, this morning for California. Corky's staying in a place on the north end of the ranch. I'll draw you a map."

"We'd appreciate it," Zach said, looking at Emily who seemed lost in thought.

The men bent over a scrap of paper. When they finished, Zach thanked Henshaw, Emily told him goodbye, and together they hurried back to the pickup. They drove in silence through pine trees lining both sides of the road. Finally, in a clearing ahead, they spotted a log cabin, and two people beside a red pickup.

"There she is," Zach said, his voice sounding grim.

Eight

The pickup was loaded with suitcases and boxes, tied down by ropes that crossed the back of the truck. Amber stood beside a tall, dark-haired man. Her platinum blond hair fell in a cascade of soft waves to the middle of her back. She wore a bright pink blouse, tight jeans and pink boots. Her blouse was decorated in rhinestones, bracelets on her arms caught the sunlight, and earrings dangled in her ears. She turned to watch them.

The moment Zach stopped the truck, Emily stepped out. Instantly, Amber screeched and ran to throw her arms around her sister.

"Emily! What are you doing here?" Amber hugged her and her perfume enveloped them. Emily returned the hug and looked at her sister.

"Remember your call? You told me you needed help and that someone was after you." Emily glanced at the man standing nearby.

Zach introduced himself to the cowboy and they shook

hands. Then Zach turned to her. "Corky, this is Emily Stockton, Amber's sister. Emily, this is Corky Powell."

Zach was barely aware of speaking. He looked at Amber, whose blue eyes met his. She was breathtakingly beautiful. She didn't look one day older than the first time he had seen her. She had the same flawless skin, the same knockout figure, the same big blue eyes and full red mouth. Yet he felt absolutely nothing for her. For the first time in his life he could look at her without longing. All he could feel was a deep-running anger at her for turning her back on her children.

"Hi, Amber," he said quietly.

She smiled as if nothing had been amiss between them. "Hi, Zach." She turned to Emily. "I'm sorry I didn't call back."

"When the sheriff called me and told me your car had been burned and they couldn't find you, I was really worried."

"Oh, that." Amber laughed nervously, waving her hand, her bracelets clanking. "My ex-husband—" She looked at Zach and shrugged, smiling at him. "My last ex-husband, Raimundo, didn't want a divorce. He was stalking me, following me everywhere. That's why I was so frightened and called you," she said, turning to Emily again.

"Corky and I burned my car to try to throw Raimundo off my trail. It seems to have worked. I haven't seen him since I was in Santa Fe the night I called you."

"That was why I came to New Mexico," Emily said. "Are you leaving here?"

"Oh, yes," Amber said, glancing at the pickup and giving Zach a swift glance.

"Will you come by to see the children?" he asked, and Emily could hear the tension in his voice.

"Oh, I will if I can," Amber answered breezily, glancing at Corky who was watching her with narrowed eyes. Emily had heard answers like that before from Amber and knew she was lying.

"Amber, go by and see your children," Emily said, unable to keep quiet.

Amber batted her eyes, then looked again at Corky. "We really need to get on the road to California. Corky has quit work here."

"Amber, they're your children," Emily reminded her, appalled at her sister's lack of concern for the little ones. She remembered holding Rebecca in her lap and how precious the child seemed, how precious both Rebecca and Jason were. Emily hurt for them, for Zach. "Amber, how can you go off and not even see them? They're only a few miles away," she said in a low voice, trying to control her anger. To her chagrin, tears stung her eyes. She wanted to shake Amber. "They're two little children who miss their mother."

Zach's hand closed around Emily's arm and he tugged gently. "Let's get out of here. Let Amber and Corky get on with their lives."

She didn't want Zach to see the tears in her eyes, and if he looked as hurt as she suspected he felt, she wouldn't be able to keep her emotions under control.

"Amber, how can you?" she asked again. She felt Zach release her, and she glanced around to see him striding for the pickup. He looked solitary, too alone. His back was stiff, his shoulders squared.

"I'm going," she said to Amber.

"Emily, I can't stay with them. They're better off—"

"Maybe, Amber," Emily said, wiping her eyes. "But I can't imagine a child who isn't better off when a mother gives her love."

"I'll try," Amber said, shrugging her shoulders, but Emily knew she was lying again.

Emily turned and hurried to the pickup, wiping her eyes as she walked. She hurt for Zach and the children and was angry with Amber. As she slid into the pickup and closed the door, she glanced at the man beside her. She saw the tense set to his shoulders and the tight line of his mouth.

Knowing that he was hurting and that the children would be hurt made Emily ache for them all.

He started the engine and hit the steering wheel with his fist. "Damn her!"

She bit her lip, hating Amber's actions. He shot her a dark glance that chilled her. "I know she's your sister."

"I don't blame you," Emily replied quietly. She turned to look out the window as he drove up the road in silence.

A few minutes later, Zach glanced at her, and even though her head was turned, he saw the spill of tears on her hands in her lap. She wiped at her eyes. He gripped the steering wheel, fighting his own anger, reminding himself that it would have hurt the kids if Amber had breezed in to see them, only to leave again. How could he ever have thought he was in love with the woman?

"Stop crying over her. The kids are better off. If she came by, they'd get all worked up and want her to stay and then *they'd* be crying. This way they'll never know. Jason barely remembers her."

His voice was rough and Emily wiped her eyes again, feeling perplexed and hurt as she had so many times about her own family. Only this seemed worse. "I always knew she was self-centered, but when she married I thought she had grown up. I don't understand my family and I never have. Maybe I should have left them long ago, but it always seemed like someone had to be there to help them."

"You see what good it did you this time."

She was silent, thinking about adorable Rebecca and Jason. She knew she wouldn't marry, wouldn't have children, so she couldn't understand Amber tossing her family aside as if they were an encumbrance. Emily ran her hand across her forehead.

Zach pulled over, reached for her and drew her into his arms. "Stop crying, Emily. She isn't worth it."

"I'm not crying over Amber," she snapped, pressed against the warmth of his broad chest.

He tilted her face up to his. "Then why're you crying?"

"Because she's hurt you and the children. Zach, how can she walk off and leave them? They're precious."

"To some people, a little kid is an interference. Amber is one of those people. You're not."

His arms held her tightly and he stroked her head. Emily got her emotions under control and sat up. "Sorry. You're the one who is hurt, and I'm the one crying."

"Honey," he said quietly, "for the first time, your sister can no longer hurt me. I feel like I've been let out of prison. I'm not going to tell the kids that I've seen their mother. It will hurt them if they know she was here and didn't even come see them."

Emily nodded. "I won't tell them, either."

"Are you okay now?"

She nodded and he stroked her cheek lightly with his knuckles before he turned back to the steering wheel and set off again. As they rode home in silence, she thought of his endearment, telling herself it meant nothing. When he reached the highway, he headed toward San Luis.

"We need to tell Nunez we found her and that she's all right."

"Her picture has been on television. You'd think someone on that ranch would have seen it and called the sheriff."

"Some of these ranchers seldom watch television, and Corky probably hasn't seen anything except Amber since he met her."

Zach watched the road, and Emily wondered about his feelings. Was he really over Amber as he had declared?

They drove to town to talk to the sheriff, who had learned about Amber and Corky that morning and sent a deputy out to talk to her. They thanked Nunez and returned to the ranch.

"I can go home now," she said.

"Stay a while," he urged quietly, lightly stroking her hand with his fingers. "You've been searching for Amber.

Just stay and take a vacation. Let me take you and the kids to Santa Fe.''

"Thanks, but I think I should get home," she replied, clinging to what she knew she should do and trying to ignore the clamorings of her heart.

"You can stay tomorrow, and we'll talk about it."

She laughed and gave in slightly. "All right. I'll stay tomorrow, but then I should go home." She twisted to look in the rearview mirror. "I don't want to look like I've been crying."

"You don't."

As soon as they entered the house, both children raced to greet them, Jason launching himself at Zach, who scooped him up and hugged him tightly. "How's my guy?"

"Come see a house we builded," Jason urged.

"Sure. And then I have to go." He knelt to hug Rebecca, who squeezed his neck while he set Jason on his feet. Jason bounded to Emily and threw his arms around her legs.

Surprised, she picked him up. "Hi, Jason," she said, holding him. She wished that she lived closer to them. But she knew that while she wanted to see and get to know the children, every moment around Zach would be agony.

"You smell good," Jason said, hugging her and wiggling to be put down. "Come see our house."

"I will," she said laughing, then stopped to pick up Rebecca who stood holding up her arms. She hugged Rebecca, feeling the sting of tears again and wishing their mother loved them. They deserved to have Amber's love. Emily closed her eyes, fighting to control her emotions.

"Come see, Aunt Emily," Rebecca said. Emily set her on her feet and wiped her eyes, straightening up to see Zach watching her. His pager beeped and he pulled it out, turning his back as the children urged them to come to the family room. Emily let Jason and Rebecca take her hands, and she went with them to the family room where blocks and bits of building toys were scattered across the floor with a strange-looking structure in the center of the room.

"What a great house!" she said, sitting on the floor to look at it with them.

"I've got to run," Zach said a few minutes later from the doorway. "A fence is down and we have missing cows. See you tonight."

After they'd all said goodbyes, Emily glanced at Nessie, who was reading her text. "Nessie, I'll be here with them the rest of the day. You don't need to stay."

"That's all right."

"I don't mind, really. It's fun to be with them."

Nessie looked at her and closed her book. "They can drive you nuts."

"Never," Emily said with a sigh, wishing she could take them home with her.

Nessie laughed and stood. "I'll take you up on your offer. If you change your mind, all you have to do is punch four on the phone and you'll get me. I can be right back up here. I haven't fixed dinner," she added.

"I can do that, too. I know there are groceries here."

"The pantry and fridge are loaded. Zach and the kids will eat anything. Only kids I've ever known that love spinach and broccoli. Bye, scamps."

"Bye, Nessie," they said, throwing themselves into her arms for another round of hugs. When they returned to their play, Emily followed the young woman to the back door. As soon as they were in the kitchen away from the children, Nessie glanced at her.

"You found your sister, didn't you?"

"Yes, we did."

"I knew from the look on his face when he walked through the door. She can tie Zach in knots faster than a cowboy can loop a rope. Is she coming over tonight?"

"Not tonight or any other time," Emily said stiffly. "She's leaving for California with the latest boyfriend."

"That woman! She's not coming by to see her kids?"

"No, she's not."

"Damn her. Sorry, I know she's your sister."

"I don't like it, either. Zach said they're better off not even knowing she was in the area."

"He's right. He's good to them and they're happy little kids. Thanks for staying. Call if you want me."

"Sure. Show me how to set the alarm."

Nessie showed her and left. Emily went back to play with Rebecca and Jason, stopping to put on a roast for dinner. Later she gave them baths, put them down for naps, and went down to fix the rest of dinner.

As supper time drew near, she bathed and changed to fresh jeans and a blue blouse. At first she combed her hair, fastening it with a barrette behind her head. Then, looking at herself in the mirror, she remembered Zach removing the clip. She unfastened it, shook her head and brushed her hair again, leaving it loose over her shoulders.

The sun sank to the horizon, sending cool shadows over the yard. Once the children awoke, she took them out to play while they waited for Zach's return.

Since Rebecca and Jason were begging to eat, they ate without him. After supper Emily cleaned, leaving the roast and potatoes covered, ready for Zach's return. She went outside again to play with the children until dusk. By the time she led them inside, she began to wonder what was keeping Zach.

As soon as the children were in pajamas, she pulled them onto her lap to read to them. Nine o'clock came and darkness fell. "Off to bed," Emily announced, setting the children on their feet. Just then the phone rang and she rushed to pick it up, her pulse jumping at the sound of Zach's voice.

"I hope you didn't wait supper."

"We didn't. I was just going to put the children to bed."

"Good. Don't wait for me. We've had a hell of a day. Quint called and said cows were missing. We got to looking for them and saw some guys stealing them. We gave chase in two pickups. Quint was with me. One of my men, Jed, was in the other one and rolled the pickup. He broke his leg in the wreck. We caught the rustlers and Quint and I held them until the sheriff could get there. One of the men took Jed to the hospital and Quint's at the hospital now. He has my cell phone and my pickup. I'm with Nunez at his office filling out papers, and then I'll go over to the hospital.''

"This has really been a bad day for you."

"The day is almost over. When I get home, I need to stop to see how the men are doing. They're fixing the fences tonight and should have the animals rounded up. Sorry I missed supper and didn't call, but we were in the thick of things.''

"That's all right. Your dinner is still on the stove. Shall I put it away?''

"No. I could eat these papers, I'm so hungry. I don't know when I'll get home. Let me talk to Rebecca a minute.''

"Rebecca, your daddy wants to talk to you."

Emily handed her the phone and watched the little girl nod. "Yes, sir." Rebecca paused to listen and smiled. "I love you, too.'' She turned to Jason. "Here.''

He took the phone and listened. "Uh-huh. Okay. Yes, sir. Love you.'' He handed the phone to Emily.

"I've got to go. See you when I see you.''

"Bye, Zach," she said quietly.

"Where's Daddy?" Rebecca asked as Emily hung up.

"One of his men got hurt and your daddy is going by the hospital to see about him. Now, off to bed with you. When he comes in, you know he'll come kiss you goodnight.'' She led them to the upstairs hall. "You get in bed, Rebecca, and I'll tuck Jason in and then come back to tell you good-night.''

"Will you leave the light on until you get back?''

"Yes," Emily said, smiling at Rebecca as the youngster climbed onto her bed and slid beneath the covers.

Emily took Jason's hand and led him to his room. She sat on the side of the bed and told him a story before kissing him good-night. "Night. We had fun today."

"Yeah." He ran his hand through the air and made a buzzing sound. "A rocket!"

"You close your eyes now."

She left the room and glanced back. He had turned on his side and his eyes were closed. Plugging in a small night-light, she switched off the ceiling light.

She crossed the hall to Rebecca's room. Rebecca sat in bed looking at a book, but she put it away when Emily entered. Emily sat on the side of the bed and Rebecca slid onto her lap. "Tell me a story."

"All right. How about *The Three Bears?*" She told the story while she held her niece close. Rebecca toyed with Emily's hair, her tiny fingers turning curls. Emily felt an ache, knowing it was probably her last night with this family. As she finished the story and helped Rebecca slide beneath the covers, the little girl wound her arms around Emily's neck and hugged her.

"I love you, Aunt Emily."

"I love you, too, Rebecca."

"Will you stay with us?"

"I can't stay all the time. I have to go home to Chicago."

Her mouth turned down. "I don't want you to go. I like you here."

"I'm glad you do. Maybe someday you and Jason can come see me in Chicago. Would you like that?"

"Yes. But I'd like it more if you would stay here."

"You're a sweetie. Now close your eyes. Daddy will come kiss you when he gets in."

Rebecca smiled and yawned. "'Night."

"'Night, Rebecca."

Feeling a sense of desolation, Emily headed for her own room, got out her suitcase and began to fold her clothing. She didn't want to go back to her empty apartment tomorrow. Even the thought of the job she loved didn't improve her mood. But especially after having seen Amber again today, Emily knew Zach did not need to be involved with anyone related to his ex-wife.

Her stomach knotted. She had found something so special with Zach. And a companionship she had never known with anyone else. Why did he have to be her ex-brother-in-law?

Turning back to the suitcase, Emily folded a sweater without seeing it. An image of dark eyes, broad shoulders and an infectious grin floated in her mind. Was she in love with Zach?

The question startled her momentarily, but when she thought about it, she knew she *had* fallen in love with him. She could only pray that it was the whirlwind of getting to know him, being so far from home and everyday things. Maybe when she settled back into a routine, she would realize it was a fantasy, a swift physical attraction and nothing more. Even as those thoughts crossed her mind, however, she knew that wasn't so. What she felt for Zach was true, and she suspected it was also lasting.

Yet it didn't matter. Even if she was wildly head-over-heels in love with the guy, she had to pack and get out of his life.

At least she would always have her niece and nephew. She guessed that Zach would let them come visit when they were older, and she loved the idea.

She finished packing and switched off the lights, then went downstairs to read while she waited for Zach.

Zach stood in the emergency entrance. His patience was shredded as he stared at the woman behind the desk.

"I'm sorry, sir. Oh, here it is. Mr. Gonzalez was treated and released. He left here about twenty minutes ago."

"Thanks," Zach replied, jamming his hat on his head and striding for the double glass doors. At last, he could get back to the ranch, back to Emily. It was the first time since she had come into his life that he had been away from her for any period of time, and all he could do was think about her.

All afternoon and night he had thought about her to the point of distraction. Even holding a gun on the rustlers, he had wanted Nunez and his deputies to get there so he could get back to the ranch to Emily.

Now that she had found Amber, she would go home to Chicago, and he would lose her. He didn't want to let her go. He wasn't going to have any choice, though. He kept telling himself that after she was gone, he would get over her. He'd survived his divorce. He would certainly survive Emily's leaving, since they had been together such a short time. But she was so many things he admired in a woman. And he wanted her in a way he had never wanted a woman before. He wasn't going to forget her quickly or easily.

He climbed into the pickup, turned out of the parking lot and entered the freeway, speeding toward home. Driving mechanically, he thought about Emily. She fit into his life so completely. And into the children's lives. Was he simply getting addled because of the sexy lady? Would taking her to bed satisfy the wild cravings that blossomed in her presence?

He should be thinking about kids' shoes, and getting the children into town next week for a pediatrician visit. He didn't want to bring upheaval into their young lives. Yet he knew they would adore having Emily around all the time.

He ached for her, wanted her, and wanted her to stay. Yet he knew it was impossible. The woman was born and bred in a big city, and she held a job that was filled with responsibility and was probably highly rewarding—she could help so many people. He couldn't ask her to leave all that and live in isolation with him on the ranch. He hit the steering wheel with his fist.

"Damn it," he swore as he barreled through the night. He wasn't convincing himself. He had seen her in tense moments, in relaxed moments. He had been with her in a crisis at the bar and she had kept a cool head and saved his butt. She was everything he'd ever wanted—and the one woman he couldn't have.

"Damn it," he swore again, clenching the steering wheel, wishing he could get her out of his mind. "Let the lady go. She would hate it out here," he said aloud to himself. "She's busy, important in her world, happy with her job, happy with her city. Let her go. You don't have a damn choice."

Again he remembered their kisses, and his body responded swiftly. He ached, he wanted her, but he had to let her go. The right thing to do was as obvious as the gray strip of pavement stretching away beneath his bright headlights.

"Let the lady go," he repeated. "She'll be back to see the kids."

He consoled himself with that outlook. He would ask her back in a month. Ask her to fly down for a weekend.

He passed the house and drove on, knowing his men were still mending fences. He found them working under the lights from their trucks. He stayed with them for another hour and then headed home, going to the bunkhouse first to find Jed Gonzalez and check on his injury.

It was eleven o'clock when he finally opened the kitchen door, exhausted, emotionally drained. The day had been hell. He wanted Emily in his arms. He wanted to hold her, to kiss her, to know she was here now. He didn't want to worry about the past, or the future.

Nine

Emily dropped the book she was reading when she heard Zach at the back door. He switched off the alarm and stepped inside, and her heart lurched as she looked at him in shock. In addition to the cuts and bruises from the bar fight, he was muddy, his shirt was torn and he had a cut across the back of his hand. Stubble covered his jaw and his expression was grim. He held his shotgun in his hand.

"What happened to you?"

"It's been a hell of a day," he said, dropping his keys and tossing his hat on a peg. "I have to lock this up," he said, pumping the shotgun and ejecting shells until it was empty. He placed the gun on top of the refrigerator.

"That isn't locking it up," she said. She wanted to fly into his arms; she felt as if they had been separated a year.

"No, but it's unloaded now and I'll lock it up before the kids are up in the morning." He turned to face her and his expression was like a blow to her heart. The longing he felt was evident. The magic chemistry between them was fully charged. An electrical tension arced in the room. Her heart thudded and her breathing stopped. She felt suspended in time, the world disappearing. His gaze drifted over her as he came toward her, and her heartbeat accelerated.

"All I could think about tonight was you," he said. "Even in that wild chase, I thought about you." His voice was husky and raw, and her body responded to the elemental rasp and the fires burning in his brown eyes. Her breasts tightened while heat flared low within her. He looked on edge, tough, determined. And in need. She could hear the ache in his voice, see it in his regard.

"Zach, you and I both know all the reasons why I should get in my car and go home early in the morning," she said quietly, standing immobile, her heart thudding against her ribs.

He narrowed the distance between them. "I thought about your leaving here and I don't want you to go. And I don't even want to talk about it now."

He wrapped his arms around her, and turned so he leaned against the counter. He spread his legs, pulling her up tight against him. He was hard, aroused. The planes and angles of his body were solid against her. "I've wanted you all day and all night," he whispered, tangling his hand in her hair. "I know I'm muddy and sweaty and should shower, but I've ached to hold you and kiss you. That's all, Emily. Just to hold you and kiss you," he repeated, a stinging loneliness revealed in his words. "If I had to wait another minute—" He bent his head, his mouth taking hers in a hard, hungry kiss that set her pulse pounding.

She had been on the verge of saying "no." Of spouting reasons to avoid problems. Of telling him they should dodge dangerous heartrending traps. She knew better than to get emotionally involved with a cowboy who lived over a thousand miles from where she resided and worked. She knew the dangers in his kisses. She was too aware of the biggest reason of all to push him away—her own bloodline.

But his mouth erased her arguments. She tasted his need, savored his desire, felt compelled to assuage his hunger.

She forgot his muddy clothes, forgot reason—and wrapped her arms around his neck. Fitting closer against him, she returned his kiss as it changed from hard and desperate to slow and tantalizing. Fires built from kisses that were a torment and a revelation. The man was vulnerable and it showed in lingering, slow kisses that made her feel desperately needed.

He kissed her as if he had been deprived of kisses all his life. She wound her fingers in the straight locks of his hair. Desire lanced through her and she thrust her hips against him in an age-old movement of need.

Zach's blood roared in his ears. Emily's breasts pressed against his chest, her curves fitting against his body, warm and soft beneath his hands. With each kiss the world shattered and blew away until nothing was left but the woman in his arms. He needed her with a hunger that was soul-deep, a passion that seared like flames. Her silky hair wound around his fingers; her tongue stroked deeply, making him want more of her, infinitely more.

He slid his hand down her back, feeling the narrow indentation of her waist. His hands slid over the curve of her bottom as he pulled her up tight against him. With a groan he pushed away from the counter, picking her up in his arms. Her legs locked around his waist, and he wanted the barriers gone between them. He wanted her bare to him, giving herself to him. He wanted to pleasure her until she was crying out beneath him. He felt a great empty space in his heart that he needed to fill with her warmth and her love, and he knew he was trying to bind her to him, to the ranch—trying to hold her in a way that he knew was impossible.

His fingers twisted free the buttons of her shirt and he pushed it off her shoulder. He shoved away her bra and bent his head to kiss her breast, taking the nipple in his mouth and flicking his tongue over the tip.

She cried out, her arms wrapped tightly around him. With a wiggle she twisted and stood again, all the while matching him kiss for kiss, her fingers in his hair.

Through the thickness of his jeans, he should barely have felt her fingers as they flitted over him, but he felt her touch to his toes. He was rock-hard, aching for her, and her feathery touch might as well have been a torch. He wrapped his arms around her and kissed her hard. He wanted her softness enveloping him.

"I need you," he whispered.

Emily looked into his eyes and knew that never in her life had she been wanted this way.

"I'm going home tomorrow, Zach."

"We have tonight," he answered, his hands sliding down her ribs, moving so lightly over her hips. His fingers paused, then returned to the buttons of her jeans. He picked her up and carried her to the family room, where he closed the door and slipped the bolt into place.

Her eyes had adjusted to the dark and she could see him, the pulse pounding in a vein at his temple, his lips looking as swollen from their kisses as hers felt. Locks of brown hair fell over his forehead. The white bandage on his temple was gone and a jagged line showed beneath the strands of his hair.

With a powerful sweep of his arms, he yanked off his T-shirt and tossed it aside, muscles rippling. She breathed deeply. Her breasts tingled, the blouse barely covering her. She reached down to pull it up, and his fingers closed over her hand.

She saw his intention as he bent his head to kiss her. She looked down at his head against her breast, and did not want to stop him. It seemed right to be in his arms. She sensed the vulnerability in him and she wanted to give to him, to make him feel complete. At the same time, she didn't want to go home with a broken heart. It was a fleeting thought, whisked away by his fingers and his mouth and his body. This moment she was willing to risk all. This might be a once-in-a-lifetime night.

His fingers tugged at the last buttons on her shirt and then he pushed it away and shoved off her bra. Her pale full breasts filled his hands with a buttery softness, a solid warmth that made him shake. His thumbs drew circles over her taut nipples.

In agony with wanting him, Emily cried out, her hands gripping his forearms while she closed her eyes and swayed toward him. "Please, Zach," she whispered, wanting him desperately. "I want you to kiss me."

He groaned as his mouth came down on hers. Her lips parted, taking him in, giving to him in return. At that moment she let go of her worries about tomorrow, gave up all restraint.

Zach felt her response as her kisses deepened and her hips thrust against him. He groaned again, tightening his arm around her waist. He kissed her in return while he unfastened her jeans, pushing them away. As they slid down, he broke off their kiss, stepping back to hold her hips. He slid his hands down her thighs, pushing away the jeans.

"You're beautiful," he whispered, uncertain she could hear him. Her body was magical, soft, enticing. He hadn't intended to go further than kisses and holding her, but they were already beyond that. There were no promises between them, no declarations of love, yet her fingers were flying eagerly over his buttons. She was as hot and passionate as he was, her response to his caresses urgent and wild. When it came to passion, she wanted the same thing he did.

He needed this woman tonight, wanted her, and was shaken how much she seemed to want him. She had shed her uncertainties and doubts with her clothing. He knew she must still have doubts. He had too many himself. But overriding his doubts was an inescapable feeling of rightness.

She shoved his jeans away and caressed him, her fingers

stroking his manhood through the material of his briefs. The moment her hands fluttered over him, he gasped. His body throbbed, and desire threatened his control. How could her faint touches, her slender fingers brushing against clothing, reduce him to quivering, breathless desire, his heart thudding as if he had run miles?

She hooked her fingers in the band of his briefs and freed him.

His urgency built, threatening like a dam to burst and flood him. He pulled her down on the carpet, kneeling beside her as he bent to brush light kisses along her thigh. He turned, yanking off his boots and kicking away his hampering jeans and briefs. As he tugged away the clothing, she rose on her knees, wrapping her arms around him, her breasts falling with a warm weight against his back while she trailed kisses over the back of his neck.

He growled low in his throat, his pulse thundering while his blood ran hot and thick. The moment he shoved aside his clothing he turned to her again, swinging her around to cradle her.

Held in his arms, close against his heart, she gazed up into his dark eyes. Her heart pounded and she couldn't catch her breath. She wanted this strong man who was from a world so different from her own. He leaned down to kiss her, their mouths meeting in a kiss that shattered her. She ran her hands across his broad shoulders, sliding them down, feeling the smooth bulge of muscles, the springy hairs on his chest.

With a groan he moved her to the floor, nudging apart her legs to kneel between them. Her breath caught as she looked at him. He was a powerful, handsome male, hard with need for her. Moonlight spilled through windows and highlighted the curve of thick muscles, his darkened manhood, the thrust of his narrow hipbones. She reached out to trail her fingers along his thigh.

Watching her, he leaned down to kiss her leg just above her knee. His kisses trailed higher while his fingers were feathers across her stomach—an intoxicating torment. His brown eyes smoldered with thoughts she could only guess.

"You're beautiful," he said, his voice as rough as gravel. A thrill spiraled in her that he thought so. He made her feel beautiful. He made her feel all woman, desirable, free of the taint of her heritage.

Her fingertips ran along his thigh and then wrapped around him, stroking, touching the velvet tip of his manhood.

He gasped again, his chest expanding, while the heat in his eyes scalded her. "Wait, honey," he whispered. "Wait—"

She heard the endearment, knowing it was given in passion, telling herself he was probably unaware he had said it. Yet to her, it was another caress that heightened her longing.

His fingers stroked and moved between her thighs, finding her femininity. She arched her hips, her hands clutching his wrists while her eyes closed and her teeth caught her lower lip. Throbbing and aching with wanting her, he stroked her and took her to another height. Dimly he could hear her cries mingle with the roaring in his ears as she thrashed beneath his hand, her body arching higher, open to him—so beautiful.

Zach knew his control was slipping. He reached out, grabbed up his jeans and fumbled in a hip pocket for his billfold. He yanked out a packet, withdrawing a condom. Watching her, he put it on. Her fingers joined his and then he gave the task to her, pleasure streaking in him, fires bursting in his groin.

"Ahh, Chicago," he whispered.

He lowered them to the floor, fighting the urge to thrust wildly into her, sheathing himself so slowly, feeling her tightness surround him. "Chicago?" he whispered, wondering if he would hurt her.

Her hips rose and her legs locked around him to pull him

closer. Forgetting his concern, he thrust into her softness, moving with her.

Sensations pounded Emily, rapture building. But beyond it all was a bursting knowledge that Zach was one with her. It was Zach crying her name in the night, Zach loving her. It was right, perfect, unforgettable.

His heat matched hers; his body moved with hers. She clung to his strong shoulders, running her hands from his smooth back down over his firm buttocks as they rocked together. Tension built to a roaring crescendo. Her body reacted to his lovemaking while her heart thudded with the acknowledgement that she loved him.

This consummate cowboy had stolen her heart so easily.

Sensations drove away thought as lights danced behind her closed eyes. Her heart pounded while she crashed over a brink and felt him shudder.

"Emily, honey!" The words were harsh, spoken in her ear. Then his open mouth covered hers and he kissed her, impaling himself in her, joined as much as was physically possible.

Zach shuddered, holding her, kissing her, knowing love-making had never been like this before for him. Emily was special, so damn special. He was stunned at the force of their loving. Not once in his life had lovemaking been what it was tonight. And he knew it went far beyond physical mating for him. He wanted to wrap his arms around her and keep her close to him always. Emily was unique, special—all that he had suspected she would be and more than he had imagined.

When she had walked out of the dark into his life, she had brought with her so much warmth that he had thawed. Before that he had been numb, hurt, locked away with his children, trying to keep his hurt from hurting them. He was wounded, lonesome, feeling a failure at the most important thing in his life—his family. Emily had made him feel alive, made him want her. He was a man again, human, feeling.

He had become aware of this swiftly. *Everything* with her had happened swiftly. But he had known from the first that he would have to let her go back to her city and her job.

He kissed her hard again, wondering if he would ever survive the hurt when she left.

Their bodies still joined, he tried to keep his full weight from crushing her. Their bodies were damp, heat radiating from them, as he showered light kisses over her face, her cheeks, her temple, down to her jaw. Holding her close, he turned them on their sides and stroked her face, pushing her damp ringlets back from her cheek and off her slender neck.

"You're beautiful, honey."

"You're crazy, but I'm glad you think so. My sister's the beau—"

He placed his finger over her lips. "Shh. You're the most beautiful woman I know," he said quietly. "You're beautiful, too, on the inside where it really counts. Your warm heart, your giving nature—you're sunshine in my cold life. And in my children's, too."

"Zach," she whispered, overwhelmed, knowing he was adding so much to her lonely life. "I'm astonished—so glad."

Lightly, she brushed her hands over his cheek, into his hair.

For the past hour, she had given herself completely—heart, body and soul. Filled with wonderment about her feelings for him, she simply stroked his face.

"Are we in your front room?"

"Yes," he answered with a lopsided grin. "And I'm muddy and I should have showered and taken you to my soft bed—at least, it's soft compared to this floor. But I couldn't wait. As it was, I felt as if I had waited an eternity," he said, becoming serious as he wound his fingers in her hair. "Let's go up and shower together."

"We shouldn't! Suppose someone needs you."

"Suppose they wait until I get out of the shower." He rolled away and stood, bending down to swing her up into his arms, their bodies warm against each other.

"Zach! Don't you dare carry me upstairs like this without a stitch of clothing on!"

He chuckled softly. "Prude." He set her on her feet and yanked on his jeans. "Now, put on your shirt and you'll be covered enough to get by."

"I will not!" she exclaimed, trying to refasten her bra. He reached out, flicked the clasp open with a twist of his fingers, slipped it off her and stuffed it into his jeans pocket.

"Just pull on a shirt, Chicago. Don't complicate life. And don't keep dawdling or I'll carry you like that."

"I believe you mean it," she said, half annoyed, half amused. She yanked on her blouse and waved her hand. "This doesn't cover me." She stepped into her jeans. Before she could button them, he swung her into his arms and headed for the door.

"Zach Durham, put me down," she ordered, kicking her feet. "My underclothes are back there on the floor with yours and—"

"So what? I'll get them in the morning. I'm the first one up, honey. Cool it and enjoy a man carrying you up all these steps."

"You're stubborn, strong-willed, arrogant—" His dark eyes were on her and her voice softened. "Sexy, impossible, handsome."

He grinned. "That's a first! I've been called a lot of things, but handsome? I adore it that you think so. You may be a little myopic."

She noticed he was not out of breath as they reached the top of the stairs and she ran her fingers along his arm. "My goodness, you're strong," she drawled in exaggeration.

"I better be to run this damn ranch. Honey, I carry calves that are five times your weight."

"I can't argue that one. I have no idea what a calf weighs, but I suspect you exaggerate." They looked at each other, and he smiled at the same time she did. He leaned forward to kiss her hungrily and she pushed against him.

"Suppose the children see us?"

"If they see me kissing you, they'll be happy about it."

"You might be surprised. You're their whole world."

"They've taken to you like a hungry kid to candy."

"I don't—" He silenced her with a kiss that lingered. They reached his bedroom and he kicked his door closed, then set her on her feet in the bathroom. He switched on the light while he continued to kiss her. She leaned away as he pushed her blouse off her shoulders and shoved down her jeans. He shed his jeans swiftly and turned on the faucets. "For the first time in my life, I wish I had a nice modern shower instead of this old tub."

Instead of turning on the shower, he began to fill the tub with steaming water. He ripped away the bandages from his cuts and tossed them away. With a scalding look, he opened a bathroom drawer and removed a packet, getting out a condom.

He stepped into the tub and sat, tugging on her hand. "Come here," he said, his voice again a husky rasp as his eyes darkened with renewed desire.

She stepped into the tub and took over the task of slipping on the condom, her fingers stroking lightly as she eased it down.

He groaned and caressed her, his hands cupping her breasts. Then he pulled her down across his lap, his legs between hers. He was aroused. Water pooled around them, steam rising. He handed her a washcloth, and she dipped it into the water and squeezed it, letting water flow across his chest. Silver rivulets of bathwater trailed over his solid muscles. Caught in his heated gaze, she ran the cloth across his chest, slowly, seductively, and then tossed it into the water as her hands slid over his warm, sleek skin.

He cupped her breasts, leaning forward to kiss them, pressing them close together to nuzzle them and then licking a taut peak, his tongue drawing heated circles. She gasped, closing her eyes, her hands drifting down until her fingers wrapped around his hard shaft.

Pressing against her, he reached around her to turn off the faucets. He lifted her hips, settling her on him, sliding into her. Eagerly, she grasped his shoulders, crying out with pleasure as he leaned back in the tub and they moved together. Her pulse thundered and blocked out sounds while she clung to him, feeling him thrust swiftly and deeply until she climaxed.

"Emily." He ground out her name, his voice thick with so much satisfaction that she trembled and tightened her arms around him. His hands gripped her hips as he thrust his own upward, taking her. Shuddering, spasms of release wracked his body.

As they both relaxed, his arm circled her shoulders and he pulled her close to kiss her.

Exhausted, she clung to him, returning his kiss, feeling his lean, wet body joined with hers. She didn't want to think beyond the moment. Being in his arms, being loved by him, was rapture, pure bliss, a memory to hold forever. She nibbled on his earlobe and heard a growl of response deep in his throat.

"This is decadent, Zach."

"It's the best there is." His hands slid over her, following the curves of her body as if he had to rediscover her. And she knew how he felt because she didn't want to stop touching him. His body was a marvel, but his responses were even more of a wonder. He had laid himself open as much as she had, revealing his loneliness, his need. She pulled him close, holding him while she showered kisses on his throat and shoulder.

He shifted, turning to look at her, his dark eyes full of satisfaction and a warmth that made her heart flutter. His mouth covered hers in a long, slow kiss that rekindled heat in her. While the water cooled and desire heated again, they caressed and kissed.

She could feel him stir inside her, astounded she could

affect him that much. With a splash of water he stood, holding her in his arms. She wrapped her legs around him, feeling his warm, slippery body. Holding her, he stepped out of the tub and carried her into the bedroom.

"Zach, we're wet—"

"Shh," he whispered, kissing her to stop her words. He placed her on the bed and she realized that he had grabbed a towel as he left the bathroom. He began to rub it lightly over her body, watching her. He picked up her foot and slid the towel over her instep, around her ankles, up over her calf and knee and along her inner thigh. She caught her breath and twisted, unable to lie still, feeling need build as the faint strokes and flicks of the soft terry cloth again ignited fires in her.

Then he flung the towel away. He was aroused again, drops of water sparkling on his skin in the glow of the bathroom light. He remembered protection, Emily's big green eyes watching him as he sheathed himself, the sleepy sensuality in her gaze making his fingers tremble. She was beautiful, passionate, totally giving.

Zach's weight came down on his knee as he bent to shower kisses where the towel had been, moving between her legs, his tongue starting a new storm of passion.

He shifted on the bed, moving between her thighs. His shaft slid into her, her warmth surrounding him, her movements and cries driving him to another frenzy.

She clung to him, hearing him cry her name, relishing their union, their passion and joy. He shuddered with a release as her pulse roared in her ears and she fell over a brink, her hips moving with his until they calmed, their ragged breathing slowing to normal.

His weight lowered on her and he peppered kisses over her face. "You're wonderful, Chicago."

She smiled at him. "Zach, we're in a very wet bed."

He grinned and shifted, getting to his feet. After toweling off, he scooped her up easily and slipped them both beneath the covers.

He turned to hold her in his arms, fitting her against him. "Now, lady, we're dry, warm and unbelievably happy."

She ducked her head against his neck, knowing how fleeting and temporary that happiness was, yet not wanting to think yet about parting. A few more hours, just a few hours she wanted to lie in his arms and feel as if she could stay forever.

His hands stroked her back, and warmth from his body heated hers. He found her chin and tipped her face up to his, his gaze searching. "Why so solemn?"

"I'm stunned, exhausted, blissful because your arms are around me," she answered seriously, feeling the world already beginning to intrude. Passion had shut them away from the future but now the clock was ticking away the minutes. The cold knowledge that she could not stay in his life was a specter rising between them.

She ran her finger along his jaw, feeling the stubble of his beard.

"Sorry I didn't shave or shower first. You may have a little whisker burn there," he said, stroking her cheek with his fingertips. She felt the rough calluses of his hands and turned her head to kiss his palm. He brushed feathery kisses over her lips, her face. "I can't let go of you."

"You'll have to sometime."

He rose on one elbow to gaze down at her, while his hand played in her hair. "You want to go home to Chicago, don't you?"

Ten

Zach knew before she answered what she would tell him. Pain started deep inside. He told himself that he had known all along that she wanted to go home to her city and her job, but his heart hadn't listened to his mind. He leaned down, kissing her hard, and wrapped his arms around her. He pulled her closer, feeling her arms lock around him and her breath lightly fan his chest. He could feel her heartbeat. He needed her, wanted her, felt as if he couldn't survive without her.

His breakup with Amber hadn't been this way. He'd been unhappy, yet resigned. He'd hurt for his failure, and he'd been more devastated for the hurt that failure inflicted on his kids. But never before had he hurt the way his heart did now.

He had wanted Amber to stay because she was the mother of his children. At some time he had loved her—or thought he had. Looking back now, he suspected it was infatuation and lust between them. He had never once felt he needed her to survive, to fill the gaps in his life, to be a companion to him.

He had sworn he wouldn't compare the sisters, but he couldn't avoid the marvel of loving Emily. This night had been the most passionate of his life. A chemistry burned between them and she was so giving of herself that loving her made him feel whole. Maybe it was because his heart was completely involved for the first time in his life.

"Ahh, Chicago," he whispered, the words ragged as pain twisted in him. "I want you here in my arms more than anything."

Zach's words burned like a brand into her heart. Emily held him tightly, her head pressed against his warm chest while she listened to the steady beat of his heart. More than anything she wanted to stay in his arms. She loved this strong, tough man who had a vulnerable side, but she knew she wasn't the right woman to become part of his life. He needed a woman with no ties to Amber. A woman whose bloodline was good. A woman who knew what a family was all about, not a woman like Emily whose entire family was messed up.

Emily suspected his desperate need for loving was the result of seeing Amber earlier; it had dredged up all the old hurts in his mind. His loneliness might have overwhelmed him.

She stroked his shoulder, memorizing his body, knowing she would dream about him, ache for him. But she knew she should go home to Chicago.

"I love you, Zach."

His arms tightened around her. "Ahh, Emily—"

She placed her fingers on his lips, stopping his words. "I have to go home. I shouldn't even stay in your bed tonight. You know Rebecca will probably come looking for me."

"She's taken to you as fast as I have," he whispered. "Don't move." He got up and crossed the room to a bureau. Moonlight spilled through the window over him and she drew her breath, her body responding to the sight of his. He was a magnificent naked male: virile and muscled. He yanked a T-shirt and briefs from a drawer.

"Here, my T-shirt will cover you enough." He returned to bed, tossed her the shirt and pulled on his briefs. As he slid beneath the covers again, she pulled the shirt down. "Damn, I liked it better with your bare skin against me." His hand slid down to the end of the T-shirt, stroking her bottom. "I'm going to try to talk you into staying, Chicago," he said softly. "I know I should let you go, but I don't want to."

"I have to, Zach. And you won't mind later. You'll see, someday, that I'm right."

"Like hell," he said, holding her pressed tightly against him, his long legs entwined with hers. "I want to love you all night long." She could feel his body change, feel his shaft thicken and press against her—and talk of parting ended.

During the night Emily disentangled herself from Zach's arms and slipped out of his bedroom, going to look at Jason and then Rebecca. Both children slept. Emily brushed Rebecca's curls from her face and bent down to kiss her cheek, then wiped tears from her own cheeks. She loved these children and Zach with all her heart. And because she loved them, she knew she should get out of their lives.

With her vision blurred by tears, Emily went to her room and slid into a cool, empty bed. She ached to be with Zach, wanted to be in his arms, knowing in a few hours she had to drive away and leave him to get on with his life.

And she had complete conviction he *would* get on with it now. He had been on the rebound from Amber, hurting, shut away from everyone. Maybe now, having let down so many barriers, he would start to get out again. She knew he would find the right woman to fill the needs in his life.

It hurt beyond belief to think of leaving him, yet she saw no choice. And he hadn't asked for a long-term commitment. He had merely said he wanted her to stay.

Tears fell unheeded this time.

Before sunrise, Zach headed for the barns. Everyone was asleep in the house and he wanted to get outside and think. He knew Emily was going home. At most he might talk her into another day or two. But then she would leave. He had planned to let her go, but damn it, she was the woman he wanted in his life forever. He decided he wasn't going to let her go without a fight.

He should forget it. She wouldn't be happy here and he might be bringing more trouble into his life. He rubbed the back of his neck and then strode to the barn door to swing it open. He fed the horses, then led them outside into the corral, moving automatically while he debated with himself, one minute deciding to do the sensible thing and let her go, the next arguing with himself to try to persuade her to stay.

By the time the sun was high and he had inquired about Jed, checked on cows and calves, fed animals and looked at fences, he was no more decided about his future than before. He headed home, knowing he wasn't going to let this day drift by without being with her.

He found Nessie with the kids in the backyard and he stopped to talk to them for a few minutes. Then he headed for the house, striding across the yard, trying to decide what he wanted for his future. He knew it was Emily. He wanted her with him. He didn't want her to leave. The house had been cold, empty without her.

Did he have a right to ask her to stay? Zach rubbed his neck again, pondering the question. He couldn't give her the things she would have at home in Chicago. He had two small rambunctious children, debts, an ailing father to care for and a ranch to run.

"Let the lady go!" he snarled to himself. "Let her go home to her busy, fulfilling life and, someday, a man who can give her more."

He thought about the way she was with Rebecca and

Jason, and clamped his lips together. The children got along with him. And Nessie was around. They didn't need Emily to make their lives complete.

But *he* did. Every time he thought about letting her go, he hurt.

"The lady can come back. She could fly here next week if she wanted."

That wasn't what *he* wanted.

Once inside the house, he stood in his hallway at the foot of the stairs and looked up at her partially open door. He knew she must be up there packing, preparing to go. With a quickened pulse, he took the stairs. At her door, he paused. She had her back to him, her hair fastened behind her head with a barrette. She wore jeans, a red T-shirt and socks. Her shoes were kicked off as she folded a skirt and placed it into her suitcase. He stepped inside the room and closed the door behind him, slipping the bolt into place so they wouldn't be disturbed.

Emily turned to face him, her heart lurching as she met his eyes. "I'm getting ready to leave," she said quietly, feeling breathless as she looked at him. He wore a chambray shirt with the sleeves torn away, frayed jeans and black boots. His presence dominated the room, and she couldn't fathom the look in his eyes. Recalling their love-making, she wanted to throw herself into his arms. It took all the willpower she had to stay where she was.

"You weren't leaving without saying goodbye, were you?"

"Of course not!"

He crossed the room toward her and her heart thudded as he placed his hands on her hips. "I know you want to go home and I know you love your work." His gaze ran over her features. "I want you here, Emily," he declared roughly, his voice husky, desire flaring in his dark gaze.

"You can't!" she whispered, her heart pounding—

amazement, joy and sorrow all mingling in her. "It's been a whirlwind, too emotional for us."

"I know what I feel, and I've never felt this way before."

Stunned, she stared at him while he reached up and unfastened her barrette. He slid his hands into her hair and, tilting her face up, he kissed her hard.

She couldn't resist. Maybe later, when she had to, but for now she wound her arms around him and returned his passionate kisses that ignited deeper needs.

His hands tugged her shirt out of her jeans and he leaned away long enough to draw her shirt over her head and toss it to the floor.

"Zach, where are Nessie and the children?"

"Outside," he said, pulling off his T-shirt. "I want you in my arms—to feel you against me," he said, leaning down to kiss her again. His fingers flicked the clasp to her bra and he pushed it away. Then he cupped her breasts, bending his head to kiss a taut nipple, flicking his tongue over her.

Trembling, she wound her fingers in his hair and slipped her hands down over him, caressing him, feeling every muscle and contour. She knew she would carry these memories for a long time to come.

I want you here, Emily. His words played over and over in her mind, heating her more than his kisses and caresses. He wanted her, but she knew she should go home and leave him to renew his life. She had come into his life when he was in an emotional upheaval, torn apart by a divorce.

Maybe he was getting over Amber and now he could move on. But she knew it should never be with her: there were too many ties that would bind him to Amber.

Tears stung her eyes, but Emily wanted him with a need that consumed her. Her kisses became filled with the desperation to love him, to relish his loving, to have one last time together before she said goodbye.

Her hands played over him, unfastening the buckle of

his belt. She was barely aware of him moving, pulling off the belt and dropping it, as she tugged free the buttons of his jeans and pushed them down. She pushed away his briefs and freed him, kneeling to stroke and kiss him. This is the last time I'll be with him, she thought, the knowledge like a cold stone pressing against her heart.

He groaned, pulling her up to kiss her hungrily. With a sweep of his arm, he sent her clothes and suitcase tumbling to the floor and placed her on the bed. He moved between her legs and let her help him put the condom in place. Then he entered her in a slow thrust that brought her hips arching against him.

She gasped and cried out, moving with him as his lovemaking became an exquisite torment, building the need within her until she felt she would burst with wanting him.

"I want you, Emily, and you're going to be mine." He ground the words out in a raw voice. Then his mouth covered hers, stopping any answer, as his powerful body moved with hers.

She cried out with rapture, spasms rocking her as release burst in her. She held him tightly while he took her to another release, and then he shuddered, thrusting wildly until he relaxed. He showered her with kisses, pulling her closer into his arms, and his hand stroked damp ringlets from her face. "I know what I want. I love you."

"Oh, Zach," she said, kissing him, hurting more than she would have thought possible. Why did it seem so right and yet so terribly wrong? She was as certain of her love for him as she was of breath in her body, but she knew she absolutely wasn't the right woman for him. He would be so much better off to let her disappear from his life along with Amber.

Emily buried her head against the strong column of his neck, stroking his back.

"Emily, look at me." He was solemn as he studied her. "I haven't had time to get a ring, but I want you to—"

She placed her finger on his lips and shook her head.

''Don't. You can't possibly know this soon. Let me go home to Chicago, and then we'll see what we feel. Let's get some time into our relationship.''

Zach stared at her, wondering if it was just an excuse to get him to let her go. Yet he knew if she wanted to go, he had no choice. He kissed her hard and long, wanting to stay in bed with her the rest of the day and night. The rest of the week. He couldn't bear to think about losing her, yet he had to let her do what she wanted. He shifted and moved away, gathering his things. She picked up hers and went to the bathroom, closing the door behind her, and he felt as if she had just slammed a door to his heart.

He went to the children's bathroom, washed and dressed swiftly, then returned to her room. She had the suitcase on the bed again and was refolding clothing.

''When are you leaving?''

''I think I should go as soon as I pack. It should take me another five minutes.''

''I'll wait downstairs.''

She nodded, her big green eyes staring at him. Everything in him cried out to hold her in his arms and argue with her, but he knew she was a strong person. She knew what she wanted in her future. He was a man with two children, family responsibilities, financial liabilities.

Hurting, he turned and strode downstairs.

Dressed in a T-shirt and jeans, Emily appeared a few minutes later. Her hair was fastened behind her head again, and she looked pale and worried. He fought an urge to wrap his arms around her and hold her. She looked unhappy, forlorn. Yet there was a stubborn tilt to her chin that told him she intended to do exactly what she said—go home to Chicago.

''I want to tell the children goodbye.''

He nodded, dreading the new hurt they would suffer. Yet they hadn't known her long and they would be playing again in a short time. Life would adjust back to the routine they had before Emily arrived.

Wouldn't it?

He wasn't so sure.

He took the suitcase from her hands, along with a rain-coat, umbrella, her purse and car keys. He carried them outside and held the door for her. "Kids," he called. "Emily is getting ready to go."

While the children flew across the yard to her, Zach went to the car.

Nessie stood at the gate and held it open for him. "I thought she would stay a while longer."

"The lady's got an important job to get back to," he said stiffly, wondering how much his hurt showed in his expression.

Emily knelt as the children ran up to her. "You're going to stay tonight, aren't you?" Rebecca asked.

"No, I'm going home."

Both children began to howl protests. "I don't want you to go!" Jason yelled as big tears spilled over his cheeks and he clung to her legs.

"I want you to stay here. Daddy said he wants you to stay!" Rebecca cried, tears filling her eyes.

"Listen, I can come back to visit. And maybe someday soon Daddy will bring you to visit me," Emily said brightly, hugging Rebecca. Rebecca threw her thin arms around Emily's neck and hugged her tightly as she began to sob.

"Please don't go, Aunt Emily. Please don't leave us."

Emily felt like crying with them, but she knew that would only add to everyone's misery. "I love you both and I'll come back soon."

"That's what Mommy said, and she *never* came back," Rebecca charged as she sobbed. Emily gave her a reassuring squeeze, then turned to hug Jason.

"Please stay!" Rebecca pulled away to look at her as tears streamed down her cheeks.

"Rebecca, I have to go home."

"Don't go!" Jason bawled. As she picked him up, Rebecca turned and raced into the house. Nessie and Zach approached.

"Rebecca just ran off," Emily said worriedly.

"When things get rough, she goes to her room and curls up with her blanket," Zach explained, his voice tight. Nessie reached out to take Jason.

The little boy wound his fists in Emily's T-shirt and clung to her while he screamed. Zach stepped forward. "Son, come here," he said in a firm voice, taking the child.

"Turn loose of Aunt Emily."

"I don't want to."

"Jason, let her go," Zach ordered, and the child opened his fists. He buried his face against Zach's chest and cried, while Zach held him tightly and patted his back.

"Nessie, thanks for everything," Emily said shakily, hastily brushing her eyes.

"You're welcome. Come back."

"I will, I promise."

"Jason, let's go swing, or we can go inside and get some paints," Nessie said cheerfully.

"Paints," he said, thrusting out his lower lip. Nessie took him from Zach and the woman and child went inside.

Zach watched the breezes tug at Emily's hair, and jammed his hands into his pockets to keep from reaching for her. "I wish I could put up a howl and hold you like they do."

Smiling, she touched his jaw, wanting to fling herself into his arms. "You'll get over this. Now that you've been out again, your life will change."

"Doesn't sound like you intend to come visit, Chicago."

"I'll come back, Zach. I'll want to see the kids. We'll keep in touch."

"Yeah, sure."

She looked up at him while inside she hurt so badly. Her world had changed. Love had come into her life with the power and swiftness of a charging locomotive. She loved this tall cowboy with all her heart. "I should go. I can't go through another goodbye."

"No, I don't want to do that, either."

She moved away from the house and he fell into step beside her. Grass swished against their feet as they crossed the yard, and when he swung open the gate, she heard the squeak of a hinge. "You have a wonderful home and a great place for the children to grow up. Do you think you would ever let them come to Chicago to visit me?"

"Of course, I will." He took her arm. "Come here." He led her around the side of the barn out of sight of the house. "I want you alone with me for just another moment or two."

"Zach—"

"Just a kiss." He reached out and caught a large purple clematis blossom from a vine growing on a trellis against the barn. He tucked the blossom into her hair and then he wrapped his arms around her, pulling her close against him as he kissed her.

She felt his hard body press against hers, his solid chest, his muscled thighs. She ached and wasn't able to stop the tears this time.

Finally she pushed away. "A few more minutes and we'll be in the hay."

He wiped her tears away with his thumbs. "Tears, Chicago? Maybe you should rethink what you're doing."

The raw longing in his voice tore at her. "I'll rethink it as I drive home. You know I can fly back here easily, or you can come to Chicago."

"Sure."

She gazed into his eyes and felt as if she would drown in them. With an effort, she closed her eyes and turned away from him. "I better go." As she walked toward the front of the barn, he draped his arm across her shoulders.

"Call me when you stop tonight. Do you have reservations?"

"Yes. I called and made them this morning while you

were out working. I'll go through Denver and then turn east. I have reservations in North Platte, Nebraska.''

"That's a lot of driving. You're getting a late start."

"It'll be all right. The sun won't go down until late in the evening. I'll call you when I stop. I wrote my car phone number on the tablet in the kitchen and I have your car phone number as well as your home number."

"If you have car trouble of any kind, promise you'll call me."

"I promise. And I'll call tonight," she repeated.

"Good. I'll be waiting," he said as they reached her car. He pulled her to him to kiss her again, and she held him tightly, feeling certain this would be the last time she would ever kiss him. She pushed against his chest and he released her. His dark eyes burned with a look that made her tremble.

"I'm going to miss you like hell, Chicago," he said softly. "If you change your mind, just make a U-turn and come back. There are some people here who love you."

"Go on with your life."

He hurt, but he resisted pulling her into his arms again, and stepped back. She climbed into her car and then held out her hands. He realized he still had her car keys. He handed them to her and closed her door.

He wanted to reach through the open window, turn off the ignition, pull her back into his arms and seduce her until all her protests and thoughts of leaving were gone.

Instead, he walked out of the garage into the hot sun and waited while she started her car and backed out. She paused beside him. "I'll call."

He nodded, not trusting himself to speak. She backed up, made a sweeping turn, waved and drove down his drive. He watched the car go feeling as if someone was cutting his heart out with a knife. His eyes stung with tears.

He knew that he had lost his future.

He turned, heading for his pickup to get back to work. He had his kids and he needed to forget the lady. She wouldn't leave her job and her city, and he couldn't live in Chicago. He didn't know how to do anything except be a cowboy. He climbed into his pickup and started the engine, looking at the cloud of dust that hung above the road—the only sign that remained of Emily.

Eleven

Emily tried to see through tears that blinded her. She wanted to stomp on the brakes and go back to him. She glanced in the rearview mirror, but she had already gone around a curve and both Zach and his house were out of sight.

After an hour she crossed the state line into Colorado and went through Trinidad, heading north on I-25. She missed lunch, but she didn't feel like eating a bite of food. It was a hot day and she kept the air conditioner running. She turned the radio on low to classical music, memories of Zach a bittersweet torment. Her body still tingled from his lovemaking; muscles were sore that she didn't know she had.

She thought about her apartment that was so tidy and that once had been so satisfying—how she would miss the clutter of Zach's home! And she thought about her job that had always occupied her mind—now she could barely think about work without memories of Zach interfering.

"You have torn apart my life," she whispered, driving without seeing the tall pines that lined the road or the occasional panoramic vistas of snow-covered peaks to the west.

She hurt and she wondered whether she would ever stop hurting. Was she making a colossal mistake and throwing away the most wonderful thing that had ever happened to her?

She had been so set on going home, on getting out of Zach's life for his sake, that she hadn't stopped to think about it from the standpoint of her life, her future. Would she really be so bad for him if he wanted her and the children wanted her?

Was she letting her family and Amber ruin her future? If she was, it wasn't their fault—it was her own.

She had been worried about her genes, and about becoming just like her family. But as Zach pointed out to her, his children had some of those same genes and they were adorable. Plus, she'd been good with them—good *for* them. Had she acted in haste, stubbornly clinging to old beliefs about herself and her family? And was Zach truly over Amber?

Winding north to Colorado Springs, Emily pondered her actions, mulling over the past week. Zach had been tense and angry when they had seen Amber. Emily had supposed he was still hurting, but had the anger been at Amber's attitude toward the children—and nothing more? If he'd had only himself to consider, would he have been so tense and angry?

He'd said his marriage was history. Should she have believed him?

The sun moved across the sky and Emily approached Denver. Soon she would stop, stretch, get some gas and take I-80 to North Platte. She still didn't want to eat, her head throbbed, and now doubts and misgivings ragged at her.

She missed Zach and the children.

"Go home, get back in routine and see," she whispered

to herself. Maybe when she was at work, at home again, she would forget, and the pain of telling him goodbye would fade.

She knew better. She loved the man. It was that simple. And that permanent. And that unmistakable.

Was it going to tear her up like this every time she went back to visit the kids? For all her strong reasons to leave, she was ready to go back right now.

Zach knew what he wanted. He hadn't done very well the first time around, she reminded herself. Yet what man could resist Amber? Was he making another mistake now, thinking he was in love with her when he was vulnerable and on the rebound? She couldn't help but feel Zach might have learned some things from the first time and matured a little as well.

At the thought of his lonely life, her pain mushroomed. He lived for his kids, but he was young and healthy and needed his own life, too.

Hot tears stung her eyes and she bit her lip, the paving becoming wavy in her vision. "Zach, I love you," she whispered, wondering if with every mile she drove, she was destroying something wonderful.

Zach was repairing a fence, working automatically without thinking about what he was doing. His mind was on Emily. He already missed her and dreaded going home without her.

He wanted to fly to Chicago this weekend and talk to her again. By then she would be back in her apartment and would have had time to think things over. And he wanted to see where she lived. Hell, why didn't he admit it—he wanted to be with her. He wanted her now. He wanted to marry her.

As soon as he got back to the house, he would call and make flight reservations. And when Emily called from North Platte, he could tell her his plans. Only it didn't make him feel much better to know he would see her this weekend. He wanted her in his house, in his bed, in his arms tonight.

He inhaled deeply, then stood to survey his land. Aspen leaves glittered in the sunlight, rustling as they twisted in the slight breeze. Brown and white Hereford cattle grazed in the distance and the air was fresh, the sky a clear blue overhead. He loved the land, working outside, dealing with ranch life. He couldn't give it up and move to a city. He wouldn't know what to do. And the ranch would be good for the kids as they grew.

It would be so damned good if Emily had stayed to become part of it.

He clamped his jaw closed and picked up his tools to put them in his truck. As he fastened down the lid of the tool chest, his pager buzzed. He switched it off, then went to the front of the pickup to get his cellular phone to call home, holding his breath and praying that something hadn't happened to one of the children. Nessie wouldn't call unless it was an emergency.

"Nessie, it's Zach."

"Sorry to page you," she answered, and his heart thudded. He could tell from her voice that she was upset.

"Zach, I can't find Rebecca. I'm afraid she's run away somewhere because she was upset over Emily leaving."

"Oh, damn," he said, sliding behind the wheel and turning on the ignition. He grabbed the open door and slammed it shut as he headed for home. His heart pounded in fear as he thought of the deep holes in the creek, the snakes on the ranch, the many dangers to a child.

"I'll keep looking for her, but this is a big ranch and I thought you should know," Nessie said. "Zach, I'm so sorry. I thought she was in her room with her blanket and I played with Jason for a long time before I went to check on her."

"Don't blame yourself. She could have slipped out while I was there, too. We'll find her," he said with determination, but he felt chilled as he bounced over rough ground and sped as fast as he dared toward the ranch road. "I'll be right home. Page Quint and tell him so he can pass the word, and ask him to come in and help me search for her. If I don't find her within the hour, I want all the men to help me look. There are too many places here where she can get hurt."

"I've searched this house over and I went down to the barn and looked. As soon as we hang up, I thought I would go back to the barn."

"I'll be right there to search the barn. You look in the yard, then put Jason in his stroller and walk down the road a little. Don't go too far."

"I won't. I'll try to get Quint now."

"Thanks." Zach switched the phone off and hunched over the steering wheel, praying that Rebecca was in the barn. The children never ventured far from the house and barn. Rebecca could so easily lose her bearings, and she was too young to be out alone. He glanced at his watch: it was after four o'clock. Dark would come in another four hours and that wasn't long if Rebecca had run away when Emily left.

He leaned forward, his gaze sweeping the land. He didn't want to go racing past her, even though common sense told him he was too far from the house for Rebecca to be anywhere nearby.

An hour later when they still hadn't located Rebecca, Zach drew a map, dividing up the ranch land. It lay across his kitchen table and the men stood around while he assigned a search section to each one.

He looked up at the gathering. "Get back here by half-past seven. If we haven't found her by then, I'll call the sheriff."

Across the kitchen, Nessie cooked while Jason solemnly sucked on his thumb, watching Zach. When Nessie glanced around, her face was creased in a frown and her eyes were clouded with worry. Zach ran his fingers through his hair. "I'll take the creek area to the east," he said, standing and jamming his hat on his head. He picked up a rifle. "Fire three shots if you need help. One shot if you find her. We'll go on horses or foot, whichever way you can work best. She couldn't have gotten too far," he said, yet the words had a hollow ring in his ears. She could have gotten too far, and he knew it. He just prayed she hadn't, and that they could find her before dark.

"Thanks," he said, and the men nodded as they filed out of the kitchen. He noticed that Quint paused to give Nessie a hug. As Quint left, Zach met Nessie's worried gaze. "Don't worry. We'll find her."

"Where's 'Becca?" Jason asked, his lip quivering and his voice sounding uncertain. "I want 'Becca."

"She's left the house," Zach said, kneeling down in front of Jason and holding his son's shoulders lightly. "You both should always stay in the house or yard unless you're with me or one of the other grown-ups. Just remember that, Jason. You can get lost."

"Is 'Becca lost?"

"She might be," Zach said solemnly, "but we're going to find her. Be a good boy."

"Yes, sir."

Zach hugged him and stood. Then he looked at Nessie, who bit her lip.

"Don't worry," he said again, and wished he could take his own advice. He strode toward the door, saying a silent prayer for Rebecca's safety.

Emily reached the outskirts of Denver. As soon as she left the city, she would turn her back on the mountains that were already in the distance and cross the plains of Nebraska. From here on, she knew she would feel more separated than ever from Zach.

In a busy lane of traffic she slowed and turned into a gas station. It was her first stop since leaving the ranch, and she stepped out to pump gas and to stretch. As she watched the numbers total fast on the pump, she held a hand over her head and stretched. Her thoughts still on Zach, she looked across the road at the hazy blue mountains outlined against the horizon. With every mile she drove, she missed him more.

Her cellular phone lay on the seat of the car. She was tempted to call, just to hear his voice and to try to erase the feeling that she had said goodbye forever to the feelings that had blossomed between them.

Yet she knew when she had driven away, she had expected it to be an end to the relationship she had discovered with Zach. Only now with every hour she was becoming more convinced that she was making a mistake.

She went inside, paid for the gas, stopped in the restroom, purchased a bottle of fruit juice and then returned to the car.

She slid onto the seat and buckled up, then locked her door and turned on the ignition. She drove slowly toward the street, glancing again at her phone, thinking about Zach coming in from work, eating supper with the children and then going out to play with them. Would he lie on the grass again and watch the clouds?

She suspected he wouldn't.

Deciding to call him from North Platte, she resisted the phone for now. As she entered traffic, she slowed for a red light and heard a scrape behind her. Frowning, she glanced around. In her peripheral vision something moved behind her.

Someone was in her car.

Startled and frightened, she whipped across the lanes of traffic when the light turned green and swept into the drive of another station. She stepped out of the car and looked in the left rear window to see big green eyes gazing back at her.

Emily's heart lurched when she saw the halo of red curls. She stuck her head inside, leaned over the seat and stared at Rebecca.

"What are you doing in my car?" she asked in amazement.

Big tears filled Rebecca's eyes then spilled over, and her lip quivered. "I want my daddy."

"Oh, great saints! Your daddy will be wild searching for you! Don't cry, Rebecca. I'll get you home to Daddy," she said, unlocking the back door and then reaching in to take Rebecca in her arms.

"I want to go home!"

"When did you get into my car?"

Rebecca cried and hugged Emily's neck. "I want Daddy."

"Rebecca, let's call your daddy." Emily sat in the front seat and picked up her cellular phone to call the ranch. To her surprise, Nessie answered.

"Nessie, this is Emily."

"Thank goodness you called. Zach really may need you. Rebecca's gone. He and the men are out searching for her."

"Find him," Emily said, closing her eyes and wishing she could place Rebecca in his arms right now, let him know she was safe. "Rebecca's with me. I didn't know it until now."

"Thank God! Oh, thank God. I've been praying we could find her. I'll page him this minute. Where are you?"

"In Denver. Tell him I'll start back with her right now. He has my car phone number. I'll stop to get her something to eat."

"I'll tell Zach."

Emily switched off the phone. "Your daddy is out searching for you. Nessie is going to tell him where you are. Now let's dry your eyes and I'll take you home."

Rebecca shook from her sobbing, and Emily's T-shirt was wet from the child's tears. She fished out a tissue to dry Rebecca's eyes. "Want to stop and get a hamburger and some juice before we start home?"

Rebecca nodded. "Daddy lets me have French fries and a chocolate milk shake when we go to Santa Fe."

"All right, Rebecca. You know, we need a car seat for you. Let's stop at a mall and get a car seat, then we'll get your milk shake and fries. Okay?"

Rebecca nodded and Emily placed her in the back seat, buckling her in. "Where have you been riding?"

Rebecca pointed and Emily saw her raincoat on the floor of the car. "I had a nap."

She guessed the child had gotten into the car sometime when Nessie had been busy with Jason and she and Zach had been behind the barn saying goodbye. Emily hadn't looked into the back seat, and Rebecca must have been on the floor of the car. She'd probably fallen asleep once they started driving. She remembered passing a mall only blocks back, so she left the station and turned in the direction of the mall.

Within the hour they were on their way, with Rebecca securely buckled into a car seat in the back, French fries in her lap and a hamburger in the sack beside her. Her malt was in a cup holder fastened to the car seat. Emily glanced over her shoulder, and Rebecca smiled at her. "Will you stay with us tonight?" the little girl asked.

"Yes, I will."

"Will Daddy be mad at me?"

"No, I think your daddy will be so glad to see you, he will hug you and kiss you."

Rebecca turned to get her malt, and the cellular phone buzzed. Emily picked it up and her heart jumped at the sound of Zach's voice.

"Thank heavens you called," he said.

"She's eating a burger and fries—she said you let her do that when you go to Santa Fe."

"I've aged about twenty years since you last saw me."

"I can imagine. I was shocked when I found her." Emily glanced in the rearview mirror and saw Rebecca looking out the window, seemingly oblivious to the conversation concerning her. "I called as soon as I found her. She must have gotten into the car when we were kissing goodbye and I never noticed her. She said she had a nap and I guess she fell asleep right away. I've driven straight through to Denver so that was my first stop. I suppose that's what wakened her. Or maybe her nap was over. Want to talk to her?''

"Yes."

"Rebecca, your daddy wants to talk to you." Emily handed the phone to Rebecca and listened as she spoke to her father.

After a few minutes of silence, Rebecca laughed. "I love you, too," she said. "Aunt Emily." Rebecca held out the phone and Emily reached back to take it again.

"Zach?"

"We'll be waiting. I'll try to pull my shot nerves together. Nessie's a wreck, too. She blames herself. The one bright spot is that we'll have you here with us tonight. I need some comforting, honey.''

"I'll be glad to be there," she said softly.

"I hope you mean that," he replied. His voice had gone husky and she gripped the phone tightly, wishing the miles would be gone and she could be with him now. "Drive carefully. I wasn't able to think about anything today except you—until Rebecca went missing.''

"I know, Zach. We'll talk. I'd better concentrate on my driving now. Oh, I got a car seat for her, so don't worry about her being buckled up. Zach, I love you," she said softly.

He groaned. "Tell me again when you get here. Promise."

"I promise to tell you," she added, feeling warmth curl inside her.

"See you, honey. *Both* of my honeys.''

She switched off the phone, then looked again at Rebecca, who was amusing herself by twisting a fry into strange shapes.

With anticipation bubbling inside, Emily drove back the

way she'd come. A while later her phone buzzed and she picked it up to hear Zach's voice again.

"Where are you now?"

"Just driving into Trinidad. We're doing fine."

"I'm headed north. I'll wait in Raton at the first gas station as you come into town on the north. I'm on the east side of the highway."

She laughed, feeling giddy, wanting to be with him *now* and hating the distance between them. "I can't wait," she said breathlessly, and he groaned.

"I'd like to climb through this phone and into your car."

"How I wish!"

"How's my little baby?"

"She's fallen asleep again."

"She'll probably be up all night—and so will we with her."

"Maybe not. When she woke up she had a big cry about being away from you. Zach, why did you drive to meet us? I'll still have to drive to the ranch."

"Like hell. I'm putting you both in my pickup and someone will get your car tomorrow. I want to be with you and I don't want to wait to be together while you drive all the way to the ranch. I'd drive until I see you, but we might miss each other in the dark."

"I was about ready to turn around and come back anyway," she said softly.

"Now I really can't wait to see you," he said in a husky voice. "Every minute until you get here is agony. Does it distract your driving to talk on the phone?"

"No, because I almost have this road to myself. There's not a lot of traffic and it's a good highway."

"Good. I haven't known what I was doing since you left. All I could think about was you."

"I *can't* concentrate on my driving if you start telling me things like that."

"All right. When I get home, I'm going to look in the

mirror for gray hairs. Today has been hell from the moment
you said goodbye.''

"It's over now, Zach," she said, aching to wrap her arms
around him. "I'm sorry I didn't see Rebecca sooner, but
she was asleep. I had stopped for gas and as I drove away,
I heard a noise behind me. When I looked around, there
she was. She really startled me."

"Think it scared her enough, she won't do something
like that again?"

"Yes, I do." Emily watched the road, listening to his
voice. They kept talking until she saw signs and lights and
realized she was approaching Raton.

"Zach, I'll hang up now. I'm almost to the station."

"I can't wait. I want to hold you both."

"Bye." She switched off the phone, her heart racing as
she saw the first station on the east, and then the long-
legged cowboy in a wide-brimmed black hat standing with
his hands on his hips beside a black pickup. Sitting on the
back of the pickup, swinging his shorter legs, was Jason.

Emily signaled and turned, then pulled into the station
and parked off to one side. The moment she unlocked the
door, Zach was standing there and she stepped out into his
arms.

Twelve

Zach crushed her to him and she wrapped her arms around his neck while they kissed. Dimly she heard the blare of a horn and someone yelled as a truck rumbled past on the highway. She heard another truck, a whistle and a yell, but they were faint sounds, drowned out by the roaring of her pulse. She was in Zach's arms again and she wanted to be there forever. She tasted tears and couldn't stop crying, so thankful to be with him at the end of such a dreadful day.

He released her, and looked into her eyes. "Chicago, it's so damned good to have you here."

"I think so, too."

"Let me get my baby and we'll go home," he said in a deep voice that wrapped around her like a warm cloak.

While Emily hugged Jason, Zach opened the back door of her car to take Rebecca into his arms. The child wound her little arms around his neck.

"Hi, baby," he said.

"Daddy, I want to go home."

"We're going right now. I love you, sweetie."

"I love you, too," she said, and Emily saw Zach wipe his eyes.

In minutes he had Rebecca and Jason buckled into the back seat of the pickup, the two jabbering away as though nothing had happened.

As soon as they turned onto the highway, Zach wound his fingers through Emily's, placing their hands on his warm thigh. "I've given Nessie and Quint some extra time off. I think they're dating."

"My goodness, what a surprise," Emily said mildly, and he grinned.

"Smarty-pants. So you saw it before I did. I don't think I'd seen much of anything for a long time until a certain redhead turned my life topsy-turvy. I'll be glad to get home."

"So will I, Zach."

"A while ago you said you were about ready to come back anyway," he said, glancing at her. "What about your wonderful job?"

She gazed up at him until he had to turn his attention back to the road. "Zach, people have problems the world over. I'm a social worker. I can counsel people in Santa Fe as well as I can in Chicago."

He breathed deeply, his chest expanding while his fingers tightened around hers. "I love you," he said softly. "Let's get home."

"I can't wait."

She was tingling with awareness of him. She wanted to be in his arms again, wanted to hold him and talk about their future instead of waiting while they drove the long miles back to the ranch.

When they finally arrived at the house, lights blazed.

"What the devil? I locked up and left it dark. I'll be damned." They slowed at the back gate. The yard was filled with his men, and Nessie and Quint came forward to greet them. He waved at everyone, unbuckled the kids, and

Jason and Rebecca climbed down. Rebecca ran to the back gate and unlatched it, the dogs bounding to meet her. She shooed them away and rushed into Nessie's arms while the men yelled a welcome.

"Thanks to all of you," Zach said, grinning and keeping his arm around Emily's shoulders.

"We just wanted to see you and know everyone was back safely," Nessie said as the men filed out of the yard. "I made lemonade and got out beer and we've been sitting out here talking." She turned to Emily and hugged her. "I'm glad you're back."

"I am, too," Emily said.

Emily poured glasses of lemonade for Rebecca and Jason and they milled around, talking to the cowboys who lingered, while Nessie cleaned up the glasses and bottles. Emily stopped the young woman and took a tray from her hands. "I can do that. You've had as bad a day as Zach."

"No, I haven't. He thought he lost two loves, not just one," she said quietly. "I'll take this tray in and then I'll go home."

Nessie and Quint were the last ones to go. Emily took Jason's hand to lead him to bed, while Zach picked up Rebecca and carried her inside. He locked up, switched off lights and turned on the alarm. Then they went upstairs to put the children to bed.

It was two more hours before Rebecca settled and went to sleep. Zach took Emily's hand and led her to his room, closing and bolting the door, then turning to pull her into his arms.

She looked into his brown eyes, and her heart thudded as his hand wound in her hair.

"Welcome home, Chicago."

"I love you, cowboy."

He studied her intently, his expression unreadable. "In the car you said you could counsel people in Santa Fe as well as in Chicago."

"That's right."

''You didn't feel that way about your job a few hours ago.''

''Yes, I did. It wasn't my job that held me back.''

His eyebrows drew together in a frown. ''What the hell *did* hold you back?''

''You should know. I'm Amber's sister. I thought you needed a clean break, that you needed someone with better blood than I have. You need—''

''Damn. All I need is you.''

She studied him for a moment while joy bubbled inside her. ''I was afraid you were on the rebound and would be better off with someone else—later.''

''You really don't mind giving up your city life and your exciting job to live out here with us and the horses and cows?''

''You're sure, really sure you *want* me?''

''I'm positive and I'll spend eternity showing you. I want to marry you and it will be for keeps. Marry me, Emily.''

''Yes! I love *you*—not a city, not a job. Just two kids and a cowboy and all the horses and cows that go with you.''

He gave her a lopsided grin. ''Make the wedding soon. Only this time I get married in a church.''

''Damn right, you do.''

''And you can have the fanciest dress you want. I'll warn you now, my family will descend like a swarm of locusts.''

She felt a flutter of inadequacy. ''Mine won't attend and you wouldn't want them to if they could. Zach, there's so much wrong with my background—''

''Shh, Chicago. There's nothing wrong with *you* and that's what counts. I just don't want my kin to overwhelm you. Now let's see all that executive efficiency at work. How fast can we have this wedding?''

She thought a moment and took a deep breath as she gazed into his eyes. ''How about three weeks from now?''

He grinned. ''That's my girl! It's three weeks too long, but I want to do everything right.''

"Don't expect perfection."

"All I hope for is love, and what we've started to discover in each other," he said softly.

"Zach, I can't believe it! I've wanted you so badly. I've been afraid to think about staying—"

"Tell me in a little while," he said, his mouth covering hers and his tongue thrusting deep as if he could never get enough of her.

On a Saturday morning in August, Emily pushed the bridal train out of her way and knelt to hug Jason. "We'll call you tonight, Jason." The little boy kissed her and she turned to pick up Rebecca, who touched Emily's white wedding veil.

"You look pretty, Aunt Emily."

"Thank you. So do you."

"You and Daddy will come get us in five days?"

"Yes. Do you know how many that is?"

Rebecca held up her hand, carefully extending all five fingers. Emily smiled. "That's right. Until then, we'll call you often. We love you. You take care of Jason."

"Yes, ma'am." Emily hugged and kissed the child, then handed her to her handsome husband, who stood waiting. She turned to Nessie, who was maid of honor, dressed in deep blue with pink rosebuds in her hair. "Bye, Nessie. Zach said he gave you phone numbers."

"He did. I'm so happy for both of you. He deserves this."

The women hugged, and Emily told Quint goodbye. She had already told Zach's parents goodbye, trying to keep straight the names and faces of the various aunts and uncles, his sister and her husband and children, and his brother, Sean, who was a shorter version of Zach, with a devilish glint in his eyes.

They rushed to their waiting limousine and waved at everyone once they settled inside. Zach's mother rushed to the open window and handed them a basket of wedding cake and champagne. "I'm so happy for you," she said, kissing Zach, then turning to kiss Emily's cheek. "Whenever you're ready to, Emily, just call me 'Mom.'"

"Thanks," Emily said, looking into eyes as dark as Zach's. His tall father stood a few feet away, wearing a tux, black boots and a broad-brimmed white Stetson. He waved at them and Zach's mother stepped back. Taking his cue, the driver pulled away as Sean Durham and friends tossed confetti and birdseed at the limo.

And then she was in Zach's arms all the way to San Luis, where Zach had hidden his car. In an hour they were in a secluded cabin nestled in the Sangre De Cristo mountain range. Zach kicked closed the cabin door after carrying her over the threshold, then shrugged off his coat and tossed it over a chair. He had already shed his tie by the time he reached for his bride, to pull her into his arms again. "You are so beautiful," he said in a throaty voice, his brown eyes smoldering with longing and happiness. "Come here, Mrs. Durham."

"Sure, cowboy. Anything to oblige."

He nuzzled her throat, his hands working to free her hair. He tossed away the filmy veil and in seconds her hair fell over her shoulders. Then his fingers began twisting buttons on her silk-and-lace wedding dress.

"Zach, your father was good to walk me down the aisle. I feel like I'm truly part of a family for the first time in my life."

"You've got a family now, Emily, who will love you forever. My mom thinks you are the greatest thing in my life."

"Second greatest. I know how she loves her grandchildren."

Zach looked down at her seriously, his hands framing her face. "I can't believe you really want to live out on the ranch."

"I think I can convince you, cowboy," Emily said in a

sultry voice, her hands drifting down over him, touching him intimately.

He wound his arm around her waist while his hand caught her gently by the hair. "Start convincing, Chicago. It'll be a tough sell."

"You think so?" she whispered, pulling his head down to hers. "I'll work at it if it takes the rest of my life," she added. Her mouth pressed his and she wound her arm around his neck, her other hand going to the studs on his shirt.

As his arms tightened around her, Emily closed her eyes in joy, knowing she had come home. She was fulfilled with a love and family she had only dreamed about in the past. And all because of the tall, handsome man whose strong arms held her close. Hay, horses, kids and one very special guy were her life now. She loved this consummate cowboy with all her heart, always and forever.

*   *   *   *   *

*Sara Orwig beautifully captures the mystique
of the cowboy, and her next sexy western,*
THE COWBOY'S SEDUCTIVE PROPOSAL,
*will be available in January 1999,
only in Silhouette Desire.*

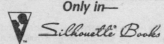

Take 2 bestselling love stories FREE

Plus get a FREE surprise gift!

Special Limited-Time Offer

Mail to Silhouette Reader Service™

3010 Walden Avenue
P.O. Box 1867
Buffalo, N.Y. 14240-1867

YES! Please send me 2 free Silhouette Desire® novels and my free surprise gift. Then send me 6 brand-new novels every month, which I will receive months before they appear in bookstores. Bill me at the low price of $3.12 each plus 25¢ delivery and applicable sales tax, if any.* That's the complete price, and a saving of over 10% off the cover prices—quite a bargain! I understand that accepting the books and gift places me under no obligation ever to buy any books. I can always return a shipment and cancel at any time. Even if I never buy another book from Silhouette, the 2 free books and the surprise gift are mine to keep forever.

225 SEN CH7U

Name	(PLEASE PRINT)	
Address	Apt. No.	
City	State	Zip

This offer is limited to one order per household and not valid to present Silhouette Desire® subscribers. *Terms and prices are subject to change without notice.
Sales tax applicable in N.Y.

UDES-98   ©1990 Harlequin Enterprises Limited

MEN at WORK

All work and no play?
Not these men!

July 1998
MACKENZIE'S LADY by Dallas Schulze

Undercover agent Mackenzie Donahue's
lazy smile and deep blue eyes were his best
weapons. But after rescuing—and kissing!—
damsel in distress Holly Reynolds, how could
he betray her by spying on her brother?

August 1998
MISS LIZ'S PASSION by Sherryl Woods

Todd Lewis could put up a building with ease,
but quailed at the sight of a classroom! Still,
Liz Gentry, his son's teacher, was no battle-ax,
and soon Todd started planning some
extracurricular activities of his own....

September 1998
A CLASSIC ENCOUNTER
by Emilie Richards

Doctor Chris Matthews was intelligent, sexy
and *very* good with his hands—which made
him all the more dangerous to single mom
Lizette St. Hilaire. So how long could she
resist Chris's special brand of TLC?

Available at your favorite retail outlet!

MEN AT WORK™

 HARLEQUIN® Silhouette®

Look us up on-line at: http://www.romance.net   PMAW2

Available September 1998
from Silhouette Books...

World's Most
Eligible Bachelors

THE CATCH
OF CONARD COUNTY
by Rachel Lee

Rancher Jeff Cumberland: long, lean, sexy as sin. He's eluded every marriage-minded female in the county. Until a mysterious woman breezes into town and brings her fierce passion to his bed. Will this steamy Conard County courtship take September's hottest bachelor off of the singles market?

Each month, Silhouette Books brings you an irresistible bachelor in these all-new, original stories. Find out how the sexiest, most sought-after men are finally caught...

Available at your favorite retail outlet.

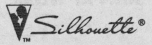

Silhouette®
™

MATERNITY LEAVE

Coming September 1998

Three delightful stories about the blessings and surprises of "Labor" Day.

TABLOID BABY by Candace Camp

She was whisked to the hospital in the nick of time....

THE NINE-MONTH KNIGHT
by Cait London

A down-on-her-luck secretary is experiencing odd little midnight cravings....

THE PATERNITY TEST by Sherryl Woods

The stick turned blue before her biological clock struck twelve....

These three special women are very pregnant...and very single, although they won't be either for too much longer, because baby—and Daddy—are on their way!

Available at your favorite retail outlet.

COMING NEXT MONTH

#1165 THE LONE TEXAN—Lass Small
The Keepers of Texas/50th Book

Tom Keeper, September's *Man of the Month*, had hung up his marriage hat, but he sure as heck hadn't given up that "one thing." And this stubborn bachelor was planning on showing prim beauty Ellen Simpson a thing—or two! Now, sweet Ellen would never let a cowboy wear his boots in her bedroom, but she absolutely insisted he keep his *hat* on....

#1166 MILLIONAIRE DAD—Leanne Banks
The Rulebreakers

Super-wealthy Joe Caruthers had been with plenty of women who couldn't keep their hands off him—or his checkbook. So when sensuous Marley Fuller became pregnant, he smelled a husband trap. Joe would never abandon his child, but he didn't have to become a husband to be a daddy...did he?

#1167 THE LITTLEST MARINE—Maureen Child
The Bachelor Battalion

After one passionate night with U.S. Marine Harding Casey, Elizabeth Stone found herself battling a fierce infatuation—and morning sickness—just days before he was set to sail overseas. Elizabeth knew honor and duty would bring Harding back, but she wanted him to return not just for his baby...but for his *wife*.

#1168 A SPARKLE IN THE COWBOY'S EYES—Peggy Moreland
Texas Brides

Merideth McCloud loved every moment of caring for John Lee Carter's darlin' baby girl. But it was high time the ornery bachelor learned that all those early-morning feedings—and late-night seductions—could lead only to one thing...marriage!

#1169 MIRANDA'S OUTLAW—Katherine Garbera

Luke Romero's rough-edged loner reputation was hard earned, and he intended to keep it intact. Then innocent Miranda Colby settled herself on *his* remote mountaintop. If Luke didn't shoo her off his territory soon, this virgin was in for a slight change to *her* reputation....

#1170 THE TEXAS RANGER AND THE TEMPTING TWIN—Pamela Ingrahm

Rough and tumble Quinn O'Byrne was straitlaced Kerstin Lundquist's secret desire...and her only hope at saving her twin. To her, he looked like any other leather-clad outlaw in Hell, Texas, but Quinn was actually an undercover lawman, bound for revenge. Was he also bound to risk everything...and fall in love?